DOCTOR WHO
THE MIND ROBBER

Based on the BBC television series by Peter Ling by
arrangement with the British Broadcasting Corporation

PETER LING

Number 115 in the
Doctor Who Library

TARGET

A TARGET BOOK

published by
the Paperback Division of
W.H. ALLEN & CO. PLC

A Target Book
Published in 1987
By the Paperback Division of
W.H. Allen & Co. PLC
44 Hill Street, London W1X 8LB

First published in Great Britain by
W.H. Allen & Co. PLC 1986

The BBC producer of *The Mind Robber* was Peter Bryant
the director was David Maloney

The role of the Doctor was played by Patrick Troughton

Printed and bound in Great Britain by
Anchor Brendon Ltd, Tiptree, Essex

Typset in Baskerville by Fleet Graphics, Enfield, Middlesex

ISBN-0-426-20286-4

CONTENTS

DOCTOR WHO

THE MIND ROBBER

For Dave Baldock
with love and gratitude

1

The Doctor Abhors a Vacuum

It all began with a bang.

He could remember that much, at least. A long, echoing explosion, like a thunderclap, that seemed to roll around earth and sky. He remembered how he had caught his breath, and how his pulse had raced at the ominous sound . . . But after that – what else remained in his memory?

Nothing. At least – nothing that made any sense.

The Doctor sat quite still and tried to collect his thoughts.

What had happened? How had he come to be here? And, most important of all, where was he?

He knew that he must have been asleep, or perhaps unconscious – he had woken up with a splitting headache. He had opened his eyes to find himself in total darkness, and, peer as he might, he could not see a glimmer of light in any direction.

He was sitting on a hard, stony floor, with his back against something that seemed to be a tree trunk. Stretching out a hand, he could touch the knobbly roots of a tree to one side, and a patch of something that felt like moss . . . But there was something wrong with it.

He shook his head, trying to throw off the cobwebs that seemed to be shrouding his brain. He must *think* . . . Try to concentrate – try to pin down the elusive clue that was just out of reach. What was it that felt wrong with the situation in which he found himself? If he were lost in some impenetrably dark forest, in the middle of the night, he would just have to wait patiently for daybreak, and then –

He snapped his fingers. At last he knew what was wrong!

The moss, the tree roots, the rough bark behind him all felt solid and real enough – but they didn't *smell* like a forest. There was no scent of damp moss, of leaf mould, of living things wafted on the night air. This forest smelt of nothing at all.

He shivered a little, and shut his eyes.

There was nothing for it but to sit and wait . . . For whatever might happen next. And while he waited, he would try to piece his thoughts together, like fragments of a jigsaw puzzle. He would do his best to remember what had happened . . .

Certainly it all began with a big bang.

Fleetingly, he remembered that this was one accredited explanation for the beginning of the Universe – the 'Big Bang' theory. He gave a tiny grunt of amusement: at least he hadn't lost his memory altogether – that was some consolation!

But this particular explosion had been of a very special kind. It had been the start of a spectacular volcanic eruption.

The TARDIS had come to rest somewhere on the lower slopes of Mount Vesuvius, and the Doctor intended to take his travelling companions, Jamie and Zoe, on a short scientific exploration, to examine the natural wonders of that powerful phenomenon.

Jamie had been only mildly interested; he said he had done all the rock climbing he wanted, when he was a wee lad in the Scottish highlands – and one mountainside was no doubt very like another.

Zoe, however, was far more enthusiastic. As a highly intelligent young scientist from the twenty-first century she was fascinated by anything and everything; space and time travel was an endless adventure in an alien environment, and it appealed to her scientific mind. The Doctor found her quick, analytic intelligence very useful on occasion – with her permanent expression of wide-eyed curiosity, she had about her the air of an Alice in Wonderland, dressed in a seamless, one-piece jump-suit of glittering silver, but she was a brilliant mathematician, capable of dealing with any abstract formulae faster than the most advanced computer.

'There's probably nothing much to see anyhow,' grumbled Jamie, as they were about to set out on their expedition. 'Didn't you tell me that Vesuvius hasn't blown up for donkeys' years?'

Zoe did some swift mental calculations and began to reel off the number of times in the past ten centuries that the volcano had erupted, and the odds against it doing so again at this particular moment –

And that was exactly when it happened.

The deafening roar took them all by surprise: Zoe gave a squeak of alarm, and clutched Jamie's hand; even the Doctor felt his heart pounding, and he gasped for breath, pulling himself together.

'Quick!' he commanded. 'Close the outer doors, Jamie . . . Be prepared to take evasive action!'

Jamie tugged a lever on the central control panel, and the double doors slid silently into place, cutting off the angry red glow that now flooded the sky. They turned and looked at the screen above their heads – a permanent scanner that showed them what was going on outside the TARDIS.

It was an awesome spectacle. A dazzling column of fire shot straight upwards from the mouth of the volcano; white, orange and crimson clouds swirled in every direction, and huge boulders were flung high into the air in an incredible bombardment.

That would have been frightening enough – but there was an even more immediate danger . . . For a sea of molten lava, that seethed and bubbled, was rolling at great speed down the steep mountainside, and getting closer by the second.

'It'll swallow us up!' exclaimed Zoe. 'Doctor – what are you going to do?'

'As I said – the time has come for evasive action. Jamie – kindly engage the launch mechanism. There's no time to lose.'

Jamie threw a switch, and they felt the power-source throb

into life. The Doctor braced himself, waiting for dematerialisation.

But nothing happened.

'Give it extra power, Jamie . . . Additional booster forces,' said the Doctor, trying to control a feeling of rising panic.

'I'm - doing - the best I can,' Jamie panted. 'But it's not responding.'

The throbbing of the engines increased - and at the same time, they all felt another and more powerful vibration, as the floor shuddered beneath their feet.

The TARDIS was caught fast in the flow of magma, while the mountainside bucked and heaved beneath them. The sky was blackened with choking clouds of ash, and yet the view upon the screen was vividly detailed in an unearthly, incandescent glow: crags, boulders, trees and bushes - everything that gave the landscape form and shape - all these were swept away and submerged in a rising tide of broiling, spitting, molten rock.

'We're stuck!' exclaimed Zoe.

The Doctor took charge at the control panel, saying, 'Not to worry - I'll throw in the over-riders - that should do the trick.'

But the moment he touched the over-rider button, a cloud of dense, choking fog seeped from the central console, making them all cough and splutter.

'Mercury vapour . . . The fluid links can't take the load!' The Doctor put a handkerchief to his mouth, and asked Zoe to stand by to give him the meter readings.

Zoe was very scared, but she knew she couldn't let them down now. With a quaver in her voice she read out the figures as they flashed up on the display-screen: 'Reading - nine-eight-seven, point three . . . Point four . . . Five - six - it's jumped to nine-nine-one - it's going up by numerals!'

'Oh, no . . . The controls seem to have jammed - '

The Doctor wrestled helplessly with the switches, but they wouldn't budge. Zoe called out a warning: 'It's reached the thousand danger mark!'

There was nothing else to be done; the Doctor threw the power switch into reverse, and the stinging mercury vapour began to disperse.

He gave a sigh of relief: 'That's better.'

Zoe looked up hopefully: 'You mean we're on our way at last?'

'Well – no. I'm afraid not. But at least we won't be suffocated by that vapour.'

Jamie glared at him accusingly: 'If you don't stop blethering and do something to get us out of here, we'll all be fried in molten lava!'

'Isn't there *any* way we can escape?' Zoe pleaded.

'Well . . . There *is* an emergency unit, but – oh, no, I can't possibly risk that.' The Doctor shook his head. 'It's only for use as a last resort.'

'But this *is* an emergency! And we need a last resort – please, Doctor!'

They all looked up at the scanner screen again; and their hearts sank. The bubbling lava was slowly creeping up the exterior walls. Soon they would be totally engulfed. The Doctor was torn by indecision.

'I don't know . . . It's extremely dangerous. You see, the emergency unit moves the TARDIS out of the space-time continuum – out of reality altogether!'

'Well, fine!' snorted Jamie. 'Reality's getting too hot for us anyway . . . What are you waiting for?'

The Doctor took a deep breath. They were quite right, of course. Desperate situations called for desperate remedies.

'Oh – very well,' he said quietly. 'I just hope I'm doing the right thing . . . Well – here goes.'

From a sliding panel in the console, he took out a small powerpack, not much larger than a household box of matches. It was black and insignificant in appearance, with a dull matt surface that reflected back no gleam of light: and at one end it had four pewter-coloured prongs.

The Doctor mentally crossed his fingers as he slipped the prongs into their appropriate socket, and hoped for the best. 'Emergency unit – on,' he said.

For a moment they all thought that nothing had happened . . . And then they looked around – and listened – and waited – and began to smile.

Because nothing was exactly what *had* happened.

There was no more throbbing dynamo, no unearthly vibrations beneath their feet, no threatening volcanic rumble . . . Just nothing.

They were safe.

Zoe flung her arms around the Doctor, and exclaimed: 'Thank goodness – it worked!'

'So it seems,' retorted the Doctor. 'Check the meter readings, would you, my dear?'

She was happy to oblige: 'Yes, of course – they're reading – oh . . . That's funny . . . They're not registering anything at all.'

'You mean – zero?'

'Not even that. There's nothing on the display.' She checked all the other meters: none of them were functioning.

They all had the same thought at the same instant, and looked up at the scanner overhead – but the screen was now completely blank.

'Nothing inside – and nothing outside either,' said Jamie slowly. 'What does it mean? Where are we? Are we in flight?'

'No, I don't think so.' The Doctor scratched his head, pondering the problem. 'I did warn you – we're outside time and space and reality . . . So that's where we are, you see – nowhere.'

'But we can't be *nowhere* – that's impossible – ' protested Zoe.

'Then I think perhaps it's time we began to make an effort and started to believe in the impossible.' The Doctor gave a lop-sided grin, and began to walk away. 'We've reached nowhere . . . It's as simple as that.'

'Hey – where are you going?' asked Jamie.

'To the Power Chambers – to check our storage supply . . . And to have a little time on my own . . . I need to think.'

With a wave of his hand, he disappeared down the access

12

corridor. Jamie and Zoe turned to look at one another.

'Believe the impossible?' Zoe repeated blankly. 'But that – that's ridiculous! It's unscientific!'

'If you ask me, he doesn't mean what he says half the time,' Jamie reassured her. 'I wouldn't worry about it if I were you.'

'I can't help worrying . . . There was something in the way he said it – and he had a funny look in his eye . . . ' She turned away and paced up and down for a moment in silence, studying the patterns on the floor. Then she said: 'If I didn't know how brave he is – I'd almost get the impression that he's – well – frightened . . . '

'Get away!' Jamie scoffed. 'What makes you say a daft thing like that? We're all safe now – the danger's over . . . What is there to be frightened of?'

'Nothing.'

'Exactly! There's nothing at all to be frightened of, so stop imagining things – '

'No, don't you understand? "Nothing" is what's so frightening . . . The Doctor said we're nowhere – and there's nothing on the meter, and nothing outside the TARDIS . . . We're in the middle of a great big Nothing . . . And *that's* what he's afraid of.'

Jamie smiled – a superior smile that made Zoe want to shake him. 'You're just letting your fancy run away with you,' he said.

'I am not! I'm going to ask the Doctor what he really thinks – I bet he agrees with me – you wait and see – '

She headed for the access corridor, and Jamie went after her. 'You can't interrupt him now – you heard what he said, he wants to be on his own – '

'This is important, Jamie. I've got to talk to him.' She threw off his restraining hand and marched out.

Jamie gave up. That was the worst of girls: you couldn't argue with them – it was just a waste of breath.

The Power Chamber was not an area of the TARDIS which the Doctor visited very often. But if the Control Room was the brains of the operation, the Power Chamber was its heart – where shining generators gleamed and purred, building up a vast reserve of energy.

The Doctor took an oil can and a piece of rag, and strolled among the smoothly-running dynamos, for all the world like a Chief Engineer in the boiler-room of an ocean liner.

He realised he was whistling a little tune under his breath, and stopped at once. It was a sign that he was agitated; if ever he caught himself whistling, he gave himself a severe talking-to. It was high time he started to think constructively and come to terms with the extraordinary situation they were in. And whistling a silly little tune wasn't going to help – that was certain.

If only he could remember the words to the tune . . . Something about a Duke, was it?

'The something Duke of somewhere – he had – um – oh, how does it go?'

Zoe walked in and found the Doctor talking to himself. That was a bad sign too. 'How does what go?' she asked.

'A little rhyme I've got on the brain – about a grand old Duke . . . The words are on the tip of my tongue, but . . . '

'You mean the Grand Old Duke of York?' Zoe supplied the missing pieces. 'He had ten thousand men . . . He marched them up to the top of a hill, and he marched them down again.'

The Doctor joined in, singing in a rather uncertain key: 'And when they were up, they were up – and when they were down, they were down . . . And when they were only half-way up, they were neither up nor down . . . '

He put down the oil can and looked suddenly very solemn. 'Of course – that's our own position exactly . . . Neither up nor down! In other words – nowhere. It all comes back to that.'

'You're worried, aren't you?' Zoe asked him. 'Tell me the truth, Doctor. Jamie thinks because we got away from Vesuvius and the molten lava, we must be safe . . . But we're still in danger, aren't we?'

There was a little pause, broken only by the rhythmic

whirring of the giant dynamos. Then the Doctor said: 'I can't tell you, Zoe – because I don't know . . . That's the worst part of all – now we're outside time and space, we're outside any kind of experience that I understand . . . I feel strangely helpless – and it's a feeling I don't like.'

'But if we're in the middle of *nothing* – '

'Then we're in the middle of emptiness . . . A void . . . a vacuum. They say that nature abhors a vacuum – and I agree with Old Mother Nature . . . I abhor a vacuum as well . . . It's highly dangerous.'

'But *why*?' Zoe wanted to know.

'Because sooner or later something will come along to fill it up again. Something will be drawn into this vacuum . . . As we have been drawn into it. I don't believe we shall be alone in this emptiness for very long – and I have a nasty suspicion that we are about to face unimaginable danger.'

'I don't understand.'

'Nor do I – that's the whole trouble. A danger that I can imagine might be frightening enough – but a danger that exists outside my imagination is far worse, because I can't imagine how I should tackle it.'

He turned and looked at Zoe, and felt a sudden sense of guilt; he had no right to burden the poor child with these metaphysical nightmares. 'Forgive me, my dear – I dare say I'm talking rubbish . . . As a good practical scientist you will be far more useful at dealing with the nuts and bolts of our situation. And I must warn you – our immediate problem is a very practical one indeed.'

'Oh? What's that?' asked Zoe.

'We can't stay here indefinitely. The emergency unit is only capable of functioning for a short time. After a while you'll hear the bleeper signals, and that means our temporary safe period is running out.'

'Oh, dear . . . And what do we do then?'

'Your guess is as good as mine.' He patted her shoulder. 'But doubtless some other solution will present itself – it generally does.'

Zoe began thoughtfully: 'I was thinking – maybe if we

were to open the main doors and go out to investigate this place we're in, we might – '

'*No!*' The Doctor's voice, as he interrupted her, was unusually harsh. 'That is absolutely out of the question. Inside the TARDIS, we're on familiar territory, but once we set foot beyond our own boundaries, we would be lost for ever – outside time and space, outside reality. We must stay within these walls; it's our only hope.'

Zoe saw a muscle twitching at the corner of his eye, and she knew immediately that her first suggestions were correct: the Doctor was very frightened indeed – more frightened than she would have believed possible.

In the Control Room, Jamie looked up at the blank scanner screen – totally empty, except for the ghostly image of his own reflection in the glass . . . His freckled face and tousled hair: his open-necked shirt and sturdy plaid kilt . . . He suddenly felt a long way from home, as he stared into the blank screen.

It had a strange, almost hypnotic effect; he felt faintly giddy, as if he were being drawn smoothly but purposefully into that empty space . . . A very far-off, high-pitched sound reached his ears, and he struggled to identify it.

Straining his eyes, he peered even more closely at the shining expanse of nothingness – and then it was as if the whiteness became a mist, and the mist began to swirl and clear, patchily, like a fog lifting.

He held his breath. It was too good to be true. The picture on the screen was becoming more and more definite at every moment; he remembered so many hot summer days in the past, when he had looked out of his window at home and watched the heat haze lifting . . . First the tops of trees shaking off the mist – then the dry stone walls around the long meadow, and the slopes of the hills beyond, bright with gorse and heather . . . And finally the great mountain crest of the highlands, reflected in the still waters of the loch . . . It was all here – shown up in every beautiful detail on the scanner – waiting for him, right outside the TARDIS.

As if that wasn't enough, the distant sound that had puzzled him at first now became closer and closer . . . The sound of the pipes; the music of his homeland.

They must have landed in Scotland.

As he gazed with delight and amazement at the images that filled the room, Zoe came back into the Control Room.

'Well, I had a long talk with the Doctor, but he wouldn't actually – ' She broke off, seeing the expression on Jamie's face. 'Jamie – what is it? What's happened?'

He turned to her, his eyes shining. 'D'you see it? Zoe – take a look – d'you see where we are?'

'What are you talking about?'

'Look! Up there on the scanner! It's my home – it's Scotland!'

Zoe followed his pointing finger – but she could see nothing on the screen. It was as blank as ever,

Jamie turned towards it again – and his radiant smile faded. 'That's funny . . . It was there a minute ago . . . And the pipes have stopped too.'

'I don't understand . . . what pipes?'

'Bagpipes, you poor ignorant creature! . . . I heard them so clear – and I saw the mountains and the loch right by my home – ' He saw that she was not convinced, and repeated angrily: 'I tell you I did! I'm not seeing things – it was there, large as life!'

'Really? And where is it now?'

Jamie frowned. 'The mists probably came back and covered it up – we get a lot of mist in the Highlands.'

'Are you trying to tell me we've landed then?'

'Of course we have. It wouldn't have been on the scanner unless it was there, would it? Right outside – waiting for us . . . Unless – '

He hesitated: perhaps after all he should double-check. He crossed to the central console, searching among the many dials, displays and controls.

'There's a wee gadget on here somewhere which warns you if there's any malfunction in the scanner circuit. No –

17

that's registering a green light – all systems normal . . . So we must have landed – like I said.'

He was so intent on the control panel, he didn't notice Zoe – who was now staring at the scanner screen, transfixed by what she saw. 'It can't be . . . ' she whispered, almost to herself. 'I don't believe it – but it's there . . . '

'What did you say?' Jamie came over and joined her, and immediately recognised the joyful look on her face. 'You mean you can see it too?'

He checked the screen eagerly – but he could see nothing.

'Zoe – listen to me – what's wrong? What are you staring at?'

'Nothing's wrong . . . You made a mistake, that's all,' she told him, gently. 'I'm sorry, Jamie – it's not your home, it's *mine* . . . It's the City.'

She had often told him of the amazing metropolis that she came from – an ultra-modern capital city with every kind of scientific gadget to improve the quality of urban living – and now here it was, before her eyes.

She gazed at the scanner with deep longing: it was like a dream come true. The City, in all its perfections, laid out in a vast panorama, with its domes and monoliths, its gleaming white arcades and walkways, its parklands and gardens . . . And ringing in her ears, the thrilling electronic music that she remembered so well: the abstract rhythm and melodies that were the Top Tunes of the twenty-first century . . .

'My City,' she sighed happily. 'And here I am – home again.'

She turned to find him staring at her as if she had suddenly gone crazy.

'Are you feeling quite well?' he enquired. 'Hadn't you better sit down a minute? Would you like a glass of water?'

She looked back at the scanner – and it was blank again.

'I don't understand . . . ' Disappointment hit her like a physical pain. 'It *was* there – I saw it – '

'No, no – that was Scotland you saw, I'm telling you – '

'The City – *my* City – wait, I'll prove it to you!'

18

Zoe moved to the control panel, and Jamie exclaimed: 'What are you going to do?'

'Simple . . . Obviously we both saw *something* out there, so that proves we've landed. All we have to do is open the main doors and go outside to see which of us is right.'

Jamie shook his head. 'Better not . . . Wait a while – till the Doctor comes back. We can't go out without him.'

'Oh, I can't wait – it's too exciting – ' she protested.

'I'll go and fetch him right away: I'll be back in two shakes,' Jamie assured her, and set off at a run.

Left alone, Zoe gazed up at the scanner once more; and once more the white mists seemed to swirl and part. The familiar electronic beat filled her head and set her toes tapping – and there at last was her lovely City again, unspoiled and perfect as ever It seemed to be calling her – drawing her towards it – welcoming her back with open arms . . .

She couldn't bear to wait another second

Now – which was the exit lever that opened the doors? She found it and tugged it into position: and the huge doors slid silently apart.

Outside, she could see nothing but white emptiness . . . But of course that must be the mists she had seen on the screen. The music was louder than ever, and even more insistent than before. Her feet began to move in response to the infectious rhythm – and she gave herself up to the beat, letting herself be carried away by it.

She was almost dancing as she disappeared into the great white void that surrounded the TARDIS.

The instant that she left the Control Room, the scanner went blank. It had done its work well.

'Will you listen to me?' Jamie was saying, in exasperation. 'We saw something out there – both of us!'

The Doctor scowled at the pressure dials on the storage unit, and absently polished the gleaming perspex with the edge of his sleeve.

'Let me get this quite clear,' he said slowly. 'You're telling me you both saw different things?'

'We couldn't have. I saw Scotland – I know I did. I could never be mistaken about that. Zoe thought for a moment she saw her home town – the City, wherever that is – but she was wrong. After all, she's never been to Scotland, so she couldn't be expected to recognise it, could she? And maybe there is some slight resemblance between the two places – but it was a wee bit misty, and I dare say she got confused . . . '

His voice trailed away, as he realised that the Doctor was hardly listening to him, so deep was he in his own thoughts.

'Highly significant,' muttered the Doctor. 'Both of you thinking you saw your own home . . . I don't like the sound of this – I don't like it at all!'

He began to stride briskly along the corridor, with Jamie at his heels.

'But Doctor – I'm trying to tell you, it was definitely Scotland – '

Then he gave up arguing: clearly the Doctor was not going to be convinced – he might as well save his breath. Indeed, the Doctor was moving at such a rapid pace, Jamie had his work cut out to keep up with him.

They entered the Control Room, and stopped dead. The main doors stood wide open – and Zoe had disappeared.

'I knew it . . . ' The Doctor clenched his fists. 'Why wasn't I here? That poor girl – she didn't stand a chance.'

'I told her to wait – I told her not to go without us . . . Still, she can't have got far – let's go and find her –' said Jamie.

He was about to run out through the open doorway, but the Doctor grabbed him by the shoulders.

'*No*, Jamie! . . . Those images you and Zoe saw on the scanner were obviously put there deliberately to tempt you outside.'

'Eh? By who?'

'I don't know . . . But there's somebody – or something – out there that wants us to come out of the TARDIS . . . Tempting us to step outside time and space!'

'You think it's a deliberate trap?' Jamie asked.

'I think it's incredibly cunning and dangerous – and in a way I've been expecting it. As I tried to tell Zoe – ' He was interrupted by a warning bleep, and a red light began to flash on the console – at first slowly, but gradually accelerating.

'That's the first warning . . . The emergency unit is running out – there isn't much time left.'

'Time – for what?'

'To make our getaway. We have to move on, Jamie.'

'But what about Zoe? We can't just leave her out there . . . ' Jamie made up his mind, and with a sudden lunge, he wriggled out of the Doctor's grasp. 'I'm going after her.'

He made a dive for the open doors, and was instantly swallowed up in the dead white nothingness beyond.

'No, Jamie – come back – '

The Doctor started to follow him, torn this way and that by conflicting fears and anxieties. He knew he couldn't desert his two companions – but at the same moment another red light went on, emitting a bright steady glow, while a second bleeper produced a shrill, sharp note.

'Oh, no – the second warning . . . '

Distracted, he hurried back to the console – and as he did so, he heard another sound, more terrifying than anything that had gone before.

It was both high-pitched and deafening: it seemed to be splitting his skull open – and the frequency of the signal was more like a vibration than a sound. His whole body shook in spasms of uncontrollable pain, and he clapped his hands over his ears.

He looked wildly around the Control Room; the noise was so overpowering, he expected to see a physical presence there – but the enemy, whatever it might be, was still invisible.

'Who are you?' he gasped. 'Where are you? What do you want from me?'

His legs would not support him any longer. Under overwhelming pressure, he staggered and almost fell, but managed to clutch at his armchair and flopped into it.

His eyes bulged, and the veins stood out at his throat and temples – he looked as if a multiple G force was clawing at him; his skin stretched tight, showing every muscle and sinew.

Only his lips moved, as he whispered over and over again, to himself: '*Fight . . . I must fight . . . I will fight . . .*'

2

The Power of Thought

The Doctor sat bolt upright – remembering.

With his eyes closed, he turned his head restlessly from side to side, feeling once more the unbearable pain that racked his entire body . . .

'I *will* fight . . . ' he repeated in a hoarse whisper.

The sound of his own words penetrated the confusion in his brain, and he awoke completely, opening his eyes.

Darkness. Silence. An all-encircling blackness.

He remembered now where he was . . . Or rather, he remembered that he didn't know where he was. He was sitting with his back against the tree that didn't smell like a tree, in pitch darkness; and he had been trying to piece together the events that led up to this moment in time.

But was he in time at all? Was he in space? Was this, in fact, the vast and terrifying nothingness that had entrapped the TARDIS – perhaps for ever?

If only he had never plugged in the emergency unit that took them for a brief period outside time, space and reality itself. That was when it had all started going wrong . . . And once it began to go wrong, it continued from bad to worse.

He tried to recall what had happened next, after Jamie and Zoe left the TARDIS, and that horrific sound-vibration had overpowered him.

Power . . . That was it . . . A stronger power that he

couldn't resist, and yet he knew he had to. He had to fight back with the only power left to him – the power of thought.

He had hung on to that last hope, as tightly as he had clung to the arms of his chair, feeling himself about to be drowned in a torrent of sound and terror and pain – aware that at some deeper level the battle was being fought for the possession of his mind.

Something was trying to conquer his mind – and he struggled desperately against it.

He remembered forcing his brain to work – to keep it ticking over – to keep on resisting. He even found himself reciting multiplication tables: anything to keep his mind working independently, and shut out the alien force that was trying to invade him.

'Four fours are sixteen . . . Five fives are twenty-five . . . Six sixes are – ' He faltered for a split second and the pain increased at once – '*Ah*! thirty-six, of course . . . Seven sevens are forty-nine . . . '

He drove himself on, concentrating on the pure perfection of arithmetic, and by the time he had got to eleven times eleven, the pain and the noise had begun to subside.

'Twelve twelves are a hundred and forty-four,' he said defiantly, to whatsoever or whomsoever might be listening . . . But nobody was listening to him now.

The vibration had stopped: all was silence.

He took a deep breath. So far, so good. The first battle was over.

Now all he had to do was to find Zoe and Jamie.

They had gone outside the TARDIS, into that endless white space – just as he now sat here under an invisible tree somewhere in endless darkness. He cudgelled his exhausted brain, trying to recall what had happened next . . .

Zoe wandered hopelessly in a world of white: white beneath her feet, white above her head, white all around her. It was like being alone in an arctic landscape, but a landscape with no land or sky, and no horizon. Nothing but white. Under her feet the floor stretched on for ever – white and shining, like a blank sheet of paper.

She called out in a thin, tremulous voice: 'Jamie . . . ? Doctor – ! Where are you?'

But her words didn't even echo. They sounded flat and dead, and she knew in her heart of hearts that no-one could hear her.

She wished she had never left the TARDIS. This wasn't the magical City that she loved – this wasn't her home. The Doctor had been right . . . This was nowhere.

Then she stopped roaming aimlessly, and stood quite still.

Was that really a sound, penetrating the empty silence, or had she imagined it? She listened hard, and far away she heard a faint, familiar voice: *'Zoe! Where are you?'*

'Jamie!'

With a gulp of relief she began to run towards the source of the sound – and a moment later she saw Jamie rushing to meet her. She flung her arms around him. 'Oh, Jamie – I've never been so glad to see anyone in my whole life! I thought I was lost for good.'

He hugged her, encouragingly.

'I thought you were, too. I'm glad I found you.'

'This is a terrible place . . . It's not the City – it's not Scotland either.'

'No, I know . . . And it's not even a mist like we thought.'

'Just opaque – nothingness . . . Like the Doctor said.'

Jamie frowned. 'Aye – he said to me – this was all – '

He changed his mind. No point in scaring the poor wee lassie any more; she'd had enough of a fright already.

'What? What did he say to you?' she wanted to know.

'Nothing much. That can wait.' He looked around and shivered. 'This place doesn't feel right; it gives me the shivers. Come on, let's get back to the TARDIS.'

Holding her hand, he began to lead the way.

Somehow, it was very unnerving, walking towards nothing. Surely he should be able to see the TARDIS from here? If he walked back the way that he'd come, he must find it . . . If this *was* the way he'd come.

24

He stopped, looking left and right. Zoe glanced up at him quickly: 'You're sure this is the way?'

'Oh, yes, this must be the way I . . . ' He cleared his throat, and began again. 'No, well, you may be right, it's possible that . . . '

He headed in a different direction, then stopped again. Zoe hung on to him, gripping his hand very tightly.

'We're lost, aren't we?' she said.

'Och, no, I wouldn't say that . . . We just – um – well . . . '

'Well what?'

He didn't finish his sentence, but set off yet again, this time taking a completely different course. After a few more steps, he gave up.

'You know something?' he asked, with a cheerful grin that did not reflect his inner feelings in the very least.

'What?'

'I think we're lost!' he retorted, as if it were a great joke.

Zoe did not smile. She said quickly: 'This isn't funny, Jamie.'

'No – you're right – it isn't. And that's what the Doctor tried to tell me . . . He said we'd walked into some sort of trap.'

'What do you mean?'

'He said those pictures we saw on the scanner were meant to tempt us out here . . . It was a deliberate plan. You saw your home – I saw mine – the very things we couldn't resist. Like as if we were fishes, and someone was baiting a hook to catch us . . . Those pictures we saw were the bait – and we swallowed it!'

Zoe shuddered: 'Don't! . . . But if something were trying to lure us out here – what is it? And where is it?'

Now it was Jamie's turn to repress a shiver. 'Aye – well – let's not be in too much of a hurry to find out, eh?'

They looked at each other in despair, and Zoe asked: 'What are we going to do?'

Jamie scratched his head. 'We've got to make contact with the Doctor, somehow. The TARDIS can't be all that far away – I only left it a few minutes ago.'

25

'How do you know?' Zoe demanded.

Jamie stared at her. 'What are you saying? I only just ran out of the TARDIS, not more than three or four minutes since – '

'But you can't be sure of that. Remember we're outside time as well as space. There's no such thing as minutes any more. The TARDIS might be aeons away for all we know.'

Jamie realised that she could well be right, but he refused to accept it. Once they started thinking like that, they might as well give up hope altogether. 'Rubbish!' he scoffed. 'I tell you, the TARDIS is only just around the corner – '

'What corner? There aren't any corners.'

'You know what I mean! Anyway, I'm going to yell for help, and I suggest you do the same!' He cupped his hands to his mouth, and shouted: 'Doctor – Doctor! Can you hear us? . . . *Doctor*!'

But at that moment the Doctor was still sitting in his armchair, locked in a life-and-death struggle with an unseen force for the power of his mind.

'*Doctor – Doctor!*'

The voices of Zoe and Jamie came through faintly – high and clear – but the Doctor could not break his concentration. The veins on his forehead stood out fiercely as he repeated the same words over and over again: '*I must fight . . . I will fight . . .*'

Lost in infinite whiteness, Zoe and Jamie plodded on, still calling, but with less and less hope of being heard. Finally Zoe refused to go any further.

'For all we know, we could be walking away from the TARDIS, instead of going towards it! Or else we might be wandering round in circles.'

Jamie nodded. 'You're right . . . And the really strange part about it is – all the time, I get this funny feeling that we're being watched.'

Zoe swallowed. 'I wondered if I was imagining it . . . I feel it too.'

They looked about, fearfully – but could see nothing except the everlasting glare of white. But now they could hear something – a far-off, high-pitched vibration, like the faint hum of machinery the mosquito whine of an electric generator.

'What is it?' Zoe asked.

'I don't know.' Jamie strained his eyes, but he could still see nothing in this endless white landscape.

The White Robots blended into the background so perfectly that neither he nor Zoe even noticed them as they began to advance towards them from the vast white distances. They had triangular heads with a single evil slit where the eyes should have been, and pointed, rat-like muzzles: and as they moved forward, they emitted that strange electronic whine – but they were almost completely camouflaged. White upon white, they blended into the background so perfectly that Jamie and Zoe could not see them at all.

Suddenly Zoe gave a little sob, and pointed up at the sky

'What is it? What's the matter?' Jamie asked.

'It's – it's just – I thought I saw a face – up there, smiling down at me.'

'A face? What sort of face? Do you mean an enemy?'

'Oh, no . . . There she is again . . . '

'She? Who?'

Zoe bit her lip fiercely, determined not to cry. She took a deep breath, and then replied, as steadily as she could: 'My mother. I can see my mother smiling – beckoning me . . . But I know it's just another trick – she isn't really there . . . ' Zoe shook her head, trying to pretend it didn't matter. 'It's all right – she's gone now.'

Jamie squeezed her arm sympathetically. 'What a dirty trick to play . . . Well, that proves it, doesn't it?'

'Proves what?'

'That it's all part of a trap.'

'I suppose so. I just wish I knew why anyone would bother to play silly games like that. She – she looked so real – it was quite hard to realise it wasn't there at all . . . ' Her voice broke, and she found it hard to fight back tears. 'I just wish I knew what it was all about . . . Making us see the things we most want to see . . . '

She turned to Jamie and began to ask: 'Do you suppose they're holding out some sort of reward to us? To make us do what they – '

But Jamie didn't even hear her. He was standing quite still, and his lips were parted in a half-smile, as he gazed straight ahead.

He could see a stone-walled cottage with a low roof, huddled under the shelter of a heather-covered hillside. It was just beginning to get dark, and the lamps were lit; the little windows gleamed with a friendly glow. Only a few steps away, the gate hung open invitingly – and beyond it, the path led straight to the front door.

As he watched, spellbound, the door itself swung open, and he could see a cosy flicker of firelight on a whitewashed wall. Supper would be waiting on the table, he knew – he could almost hear the crackle of a log burning on the hearth –

'Jamie – what is it?' Zoe persisted.

'My wee house . . . My ain folk waiting supper for me – '

'It's not *real*, Jamie – you know that.'

But he was like someone in a trance, and she could not get through to him.

'I tell you, it *is* real – they're all there, ready and waiting – can ye no see them? I must go to them . . . '

He took a few uncertain steps forward, and Zoe acted swiftly.

'No, Jamie, no!' She drew back her hand and gave him a stinging slap across the face. Instantly, he came to his senses, nursing his jawbone.

'Ouch! What did you go and do that for?' He looked straight ahead again – but there was nothing there. The spell had been broken, and the tempting image had disappeared.

'Thank you,' he said softly. 'You were right . . . It almost had me fooled that time.'

'Come on – let's keep going,' said Zoe. 'We know now that whatever we see or hear, it'll only be another of their horrible tricks . . . '

Jamie stopped dead in his tracks. 'I'm not so sure of that,' he said huskily. 'Look – *there*!'

The White Robots were a lot closer now, advancing in a tightly-packed formation only a few yards away: and their electronic humming was louder than ever.

'It's another illusion – ' Zoe gasped.

'I don't think so . . . They look real enough to me . . . And none too friendly, I'd say.' Jamie suddenly leapt into action. 'Don't hang about, Zoe – let's make a run for it!'

They turned and raced in the opposite direction – but found themselves face to face with another line of White Robots, cutting off their retreat.

They tried twisting and turning, but each way they went, more and more of the hostile automata crowded in on them, until they were totally surrounded.

The two companions stood hand in hand, as the Robot troops moved in closer still. And then they saw the most terrifying sight of all.

In the middle of the line, there were two figures who were not Robots. They looked like human beings – a boy and a girl – although they were dressed from top to toe in white. The girl had short white hair, and a shining white jump suit: the boy wore a white plaid shirt, and a white kilt with a white sporran . . .

Zoe and Jamie saw themselves – like bleached reflections in a mirror – waving, and smiling – mouthing silent words of welcome – and beckoning them to come and join them.

That was when Zoe screamed with terror.

This time Zoe's scream penetrated the Doctor's tortured brain, and he stiffened – instantly alert.

He shut his eyes, trying to concentrate, and a crazy image floated into his head: his two young companions, all in white – silently mouthing and beckoning. He shivered: this was another mirage – it had to be.

'Zoe! Jamie!' he shouted, with all the strength he could muster. 'Don't listen to them – don't go with them . . . '

And then something very unexpected happened.

Another voice broke in on the Doctor's thoughts – he could not tell where it came from – it seemed to be somewhere inside his head. The voice was not sinister or bullying: it was soft and kindly – sweetly reasonable. You had to trust a voice like that.

'*Follow them, my dear Doctor,*' the Voice advised him gently. '*Follow – and save them – before it is too late . . . Why don't you?*'

The Doctor opened his eyes – but there was no-one to be seen. He was still alone in the TARDIS, to all intents and purposes.

'*Go now,*' purred the Voice. '*At once – before it's too late . . . They need you.*'

'Who are you?' the Doctor said aloud. 'What do you want with us?'

'*I'm trying to help you – for your own good . . . You must follow them,*' the Voice insisted.

'No! I won't do it . . . I won't give in to you . . . I don't trust you!'

'*Ahh . . . But you will . . . You will . . . You will . . .*'

Slowly the Voice faded, until it was only a thread of echo, hanging on the air like a wisp of smoke – and then it had gone.

Out in the limbo where time and space no longer existed, the White Robots were massing as if to attack. Zoe and Jamie stood shoulder to shoulder, determined that if this was their last moment, they would at least go down fighting.

Slowly and inexorably, the Robots moved closer, a step at a time – and Jamie suddenly realised that each one held a circular object – a compound lens, with reflecting, concentric circles. As he watched, the lens began to shine, emitting a dazzling ray of magnesium brilliance, so fierce that he could not look at it. He screwed up his eyes against the glare . . .

That was why he didn't realise for a moment what was happening.

At the centre of the enemy line, the white replicas that looked so horribly like themselves had begun to glide towards them, growing larger and larger. They did not seem to walk but rather to zoom in as an image on a television screen zooms in for a close-up.

Worse still, Jamie realised that he and Zoe were being propelled towards them in the same uncanny way – their feet did not move – it was as if a powerful magnetic force were drawing them together.

Zoe screamed again: 'No! We can't – we'll be swallowed up – they're going to draw us in – '

But it was too late. Despite her cries of protest, the real Zoe was being sucked into the false white Zoe – and the real Jamie was rapidly approaching his unreal counterpart. He braced himself for the shock of impact, but there was none.

The two couples met and mingled, sliding into each other without any jolt, as smoothly as a swimmer entering a calm, unbroken sheet of water. It was as if they had gone through a looking glass, and become one with their own reflections.

And then the screaming stopped.

Now there was only one Zoe, and one Jamie – dressed in white, nodding and smiling; as inhuman as the Robots that surrounded them.

The Doctor saw it happening, in his mind's eye, and recoiled.

Was this a form of death – a particularly sinister death-in-life? He could not let such a monstrous thing happen without a struggle.

'I won't permit it!' he said, rising from his armchair. 'I can't let it happen to them . . . Not to them.'

Then the Voice spoke again, and the Doctor could hear that it was smiling: '*Quite so, my dear Doctor . . . I knew you'd see it my way, sooner or later. Now, all you have to do is get out and save them . . . Follow them – go on – the doors are still wide open!*'

It was true. The Doctor only had to take a few steps, and he would be outside the TARDIS – out in that white void, with Zoe and Jamie – fighting to win them back from the evil limbo where they were trapped for ever.

'*Go now . . .*' whispered the Voice. '*It's your last chance . . .*'

Go and save them – you can't abandon your friends – go at once . . . '

The Voice was wickedly persuasive, and the Doctor had no choice. He squared his shoulders, and set out – well aware that he might never see the TARDIS again, and that he too might be lost for all eternity.

The chill of the emptiness struck him as soon as he had passed through the open portals . . . Endless white – no sun, no warmth, no life . . . All quite still – silent – and dead.

He looked back over his shoulder. There was the TARDIS at least – but even that had undergone a total transformation; for the dark-blue police box was now totally white.

He pressed ahead – and then he saw them; Jamie and Zoe, hand in hand – their eyes wide and unblinking, like mannequins in a shop window . . . White mannequins, in white costumes – and behind them, lined up in serried ranks, was the army of White Robots.

The Doctor had never seen creatures like this before, but he summed them up in one dismissive glance. As automata went, they seemed to be of a fairly low standard in terms of scientific advancement – their movements were limited, and their intelligence functioned only on a very basic level.

'So far, so good,' he told himself. 'They shouldn't pose much of a threat.'

He raised a hand in friendly greeting to the zombie-like characters who were once his travelling companions.

'Zoe, Jamie – I've found you at last,' he said.

But they did not respond, or even attempt to speak: perhaps they could not do so. They simply stared ahead, glassy-eyed, without any sign of reaction.

The Doctor thought fast. There was only one possible way to get through to them.

'Listen to me – very carefully,' he said. 'This is vitally important to all of us – a matter of life or death.'

He chose his words with care, as he continued: 'Concentrate very hard on what I am saying . . . Listen to my words, and ignore everything else . . . Think of me – think of the TARDIS – we are the only real things here. Everything else is an illusion – none of it is real.'

As he watched, a strange thing happened.

Zoe and Jamie seemed to flicker like the shadowy frames of an old silent film – they wavered and flashed from white to dark, their images alternating between the dead whiteness of the zombie characters, and a stroboscopic glimpse of the real Zoe and Jamie, dressed in their own familiar clothes. He blinked, and did his best to focus on the split-second flashes of reality as they passed before his eyes.

'Come with me – back to the TARDIS . . . Nothing else matters – all the rest is a stupid conjuring trick, designed to confuse you . . . That is why you must concentrate on what is real and true . . . Come to me – now!'

Slowly, as if they were sleepwalking, the young couple began to move forward, in obedience to his command.

'Walk straight to the TARDIS – it's only a few steps away . . .'

But as they advanced, the line of Robots began to follow, and seemed likely to overtake them. The Doctor saw a shadow of fear on Zoe's face, and he said instantly: 'Don't stop – don't look behind you, whatever you do . . . The door of the TARDIS is open . . . You'll be safe there . . . Keep going!'

Now the white replicas were only sporadic and fleeting – Zoe and Jamie were much more visible, and their images were getting stronger and more steady all the time.

The Doctor held his arms out, encouragingly: 'You're almost there – I know you can make it – come to me . . .'

To his dismay, he saw one of the Robots lifting the circular lens and pointing it in his direction: was he too about to be translated into a lifeless waxwork? The light flared towards him in a steady, penetrating beam, and he threw up a hand instinctively, shielding his eyes. If that powerful ray should reach him, heaven only knew what horror he might see within the ribbed mirror . . .

'Quickly, Zoe! Jamie! Go in before it's too late!' he shouted and turned his back on the advancing enemy troops, grabbing the hands of his companions, and then flinging them bodily in through the open doorway.

The moment he turned away, the magnesium ray and the Robot operating it disappeared: the entire array of Robot troops vanished into thin air and total silence. The Doctor knew, without having to look back, that they were safe.

'Well!' he gasped, falling on the exit lever, and pulling it with all his might. 'Out of sight, out of mind - to coin a phrase . . . '

The main doors slid together without a sound. They were safe inside the TARDIS again . . . Or were they?

Jamie scratched his head, totally confused.

'What's been going on?' he asked doubtfully. 'Zoe - I had an idea you were all white . . . '

'So were you! It was the Robots - they tried to steal us away and turn us into something else - it was horrible.'

'Quiet!' The Doctor was at the central console, checking all the dials and meters. He shook his head, dissatisfied with what he read on the panel. 'We're not out of the wood yet, I'm afraid.'

(Somewhere far away, in total darkness, the Doctor sat with his back to a tree that wasn't a tree, in the midst of a forest that wasn't a forest, and gave a wry chuckle as he recalled this careless phrase. That's what he had said: 'Not out of the wood yet.' Little did he know how prophetic his words were to be . . .)

'Still - first things first!' The Doctor glanced over at the two youngsters, with concern. 'How are you feeling now?'

Zoe shrugged. 'All right in myself, I suppose . . . But what really happened?'

'Nothing *really* happened, my dear. Because nothing was real.'

'But where were you?'

'Nowhere. I keep telling you - all the things you saw - or rather, the things you think you saw - were pure imagination, nothing more.'

'But why?' Jamie demanded. 'What's it all about?'

'I don't know,' said the Doctor. 'All I can tell you is that we must be careful . . . Very, very careful.'

Jamie smothered a yawn. 'I don't see why - now we're

34

back where we started, we're all safe and sound, aren't we? And I feel a bit sleepy . . . I think I'll go and get my head down for five minutes.'

'Good idea – after all that excitement, it's natural enough for you to feel a trifle fatigued. Off your go – we'll call you if we need you.'

Jamie nodded, and made his way to his room; his bed had never seemed more cosy or more attractive.

When he was out of earshot, Zoe said shrewdly: 'You're still worried, though – aren't you?'

'I'm not totally reassured, if that's what you mean,' the Doctor began evasively. 'But at least I see no reason to hang around in this unhealthy environment a moment longer than we have to. By now the fluid links will have cooled down, and we should have built a sufficient power back-up to get us safely on our way . . . '

He pulled the main switch, and prepared for take-off.

The familiar drumming of the power supply was reassuring – and yet there was something else . . . An alien noise that seemed to cut through all other sounds. They listened intently, and then Zoe asked: 'What was that? Is the TARDIS going wrong again?'

'Oh, no – I shouldn't think so for a moment. We're on our way all right – but I'm not sure where we're going.'

Zoe smiled: 'That's nothing unusual!' Then her smile faded, and she looked a little ashamed of herself. 'I'm sorry . . . '

'Nothing to feel sorry about – you've done nothing wrong.'

'But I have . . . It was all my fault – going outside without permission. It was nearly the end of everything.'

'Don't worry your head over that, my dear. I don't think you had much choice. Whoever was tempting you made it seem quite irresistible. I even gave in myself, when the Voice lured me outside – he was certainly very persuasive.'

'Voice? What voice?'

'I can't tell you . . . Perhaps there wasn't one. Perhaps that was just another illusion too. Still, the TARDIS seems to be functioning normally again, thank goodness – ' He checked the meters again, and frowned. 'That's odd.'

'What is?'

'The levels have fallen below the thousand minimum.'

'Is that critical?'

'Well – it does mean we're expending energy faster than we're producing it . . . But don't worry – there's a special power-boost unit . . . Somewhere . . . If only I can lay my hands on it . . . '

Zoe raised her eyes to heaven in mute exasperation. Really, the Doctor could be so vague sometimes! It offended her scientific mind. She rather wished she'd followed Jamie's example and snatched forty winks – certainly she was doing no good here.

By now, Jamie was fast asleep – and in the throes of a bad dream. He threshed from side to side, his brows furrowed, and his lips moved, forming the words: 'No – no . . . !'

The Doctor found the power-boost switch at last, and as he operated it, a comforting humming noise came from the controls.

'That's more like it . . . Zoe, what does the meter read now?'

She was glad to have something useful to do at last, and reeled off the figures: 'Nine-nine zero . . . Nine-nine one . . . Two . . . Three . . . '

By the time the figures reached nine-nine-eight, Jamie had rejoined them, rubbing his eyes, and saying: 'Hey – you know what? I just had a terrible nightmare . . . '

'Ssh! Do be quiet, Jamie – this is important,' said the Doctor.

'Nine-nine-eight,' Zoe repeated. 'Steady at eight.'

'No, listen – it was the most terrifying dream. There was this big white horse coming at me – with a great pointed horn in the middle of its head – '

'I don't want to blow the storage units again,' the Doctor continued to explain to Zoe. 'We'll just let it creep up gradually.'

Zoe, trying to listen to them both at once, said: 'Yes,

Doctor – whatever you say . . . A horse with a pointed horn, Jamie? Sounds like a unicorn!'

'Yeah – well, maybe it was. All I know is, it was charging straight towards me – I thought I was done for . . . Head down, ready for the kill!'

'Really, Jamie, now who's letting his imagination run away with – ' Zoe glanced across at the Doctor, and then her voice changed. 'Jamie – look . . . What's the matter, Doctor?'

For the Doctor was sitting in his chair, gripping the arms: with a look of deep apprehension on his face.

'Be quiet – both of you . . . ' he said. 'Can't you hear that sound? It's beginning again.'

They all heard it then – at first only the merest vibration, but gradually increasing in power and volume.

'I've heard it before,' the Doctor warned them. 'Brace yourself – it's an alien force trying to demoralise us . . . '

Zoe clapped her hands over her ears: 'I feel it too – in my head!'

The Doctor tried to help as best he could: 'Concentrate – both of you . . . You must concentrate on something . . . Zoe – read the figures out – keep reading them!'

She did her best: 'Nine-nine-nine . . . One thousand . . . '

'You too, Jamie! You must both fight back . . . It's getting stronger . . . '

They tried hard – 'One thousand and one . . . Two . . . Three – ' but it was no good. The sound was everywhere now, surrounding them, inside and out, as if it would shake them to pieces.

'It's too strong for us . . . Too powerful – I can't fight any more!'

These were the last words the Doctor uttered – and then the explosion happened.

Floating in blackness, slowly revolving, the TARDIS began to break up. It happened as if in slow motion – walls, door, roof all dropped away, and the central control panel was left circling in endless night, with Zoe and Jamie clinging on to it for dear life.

Zoe looked round wildly, and screamed with terror: 'Jamie! The Doctor . . . *We've lost him*!'

That was the last they saw of him: still sitting in his armchair, falling through space . . . Falling, falling . . . Until he finally disappeared from sight.

3

Boys and Girls Come Out to Play

The central control console was all that was left of the TARDIS, and it now revolved through space like a giant spinning-top, while Zoe and Jamie held on to it with all their strength; their knuckles were white with the immense strain upon them.

'I can't – hold on – much longer – ' Zoe gasped.

'You've got to!' Jamie urged her. 'If you let go now, we'll be lost for ever.'

'Like the Doctor . . . ' She felt tears choking her. 'We'll never see him again – and the TARDIS has gone for good . . . What's the use of hoping?'

'You must never give up hope!' Jamie admonished her: but a rushing wind tore the words from his lips, as they whirled onwards into darkness.

The control console seemed to be caught in a space whirlpool: it was rotating faster and faster, and they could feel centrifugal force dragging at them.

'It's no good!' Zoe's fingers were slipping, and she knew she was powerless to resist. 'It's all over!'

She found herself being flung off into the void – her dark hair streaming out behind her like the tail of a meteor. She closed her eyes, and gave herself up to the sensation of floating . . .

Floating . . . Weightless . . . In total silence . . .

It was curiously peaceful. Almost like falling asleep . . .

Dawn came to the forest at long last: and it came very slowly.

From total blackness, the faintest glimmer of light began to slide across the rim of the sky, and for the first time the Doctor could see vague, looming shapes surrounding him.

Tall trees – amazingly tall and straight – like the pillars and arches of a vast cathedral; they were of different sizes and shapes, clustered closely together in strange patterns, almost like a maze. The Doctor looked about him, and wondered if someone had originally planted them like this on purpose. It would make a wonderful hiding place.

But he had been in hiding far too long. It was time to set out in search of his two companions. He had no valid reason to suppose that, like him, they had landed safely in this eerie forest after the TARDIS disintegrated – but since he was here, it seemed at least to be an arguable possibility that they might not be far away.

He rose to his feet with a little difficulty, supporting himself by holding on to the smoothly-ribbed trunk of the tree he had been leaning against throughout the long night.

How shockingly stiff and sore he felt; his old bones creaked as he flexed his arms and legs.

Well, that wasn't to be wondered at. He had gone through some fairly gruelling experiences in the last twenty-four hours – he'd been removed from the bounds of space and time, he'd had his mind invaded by an alien power, he'd lost his two companions, and he'd lost the dear old TARDIS . . . Hardly surprising if he wasn't feeling quite up to the mark this morning.

He screwed up his eyes, trying to see more clearly – but it was still very dark. The forest tree trunks disappeared upwards into impenetrable gloom: here and there, between the tall columns he could glimpse a patch of night sky, streaked with the first green light of dawn – but that was all.

Still, he couldn't hang about for ever. He had to get on and find out where he was . . . And where the others had got to . . . And what in the name of goodness was going on.

Squaring his shoulders, he strode ahead into the maze.

If anyone could have had a bird's-eye view of the scene, he might have been amazed to see the three time-travellers, all making separate efforts to find their way through the forest.

This way and that, they twisted and turned among the tall trees – so near to one another, and yet so far apart. The Doctor trudged onwards in a straight line – or as near straight as he could manage, avoiding the obstacles in his path – with a vague intention of heading for the slowly-increasing greenish glow of early morning, somewhere far ahead.

Jamie zig-zagged from side to side, going first this way, then that, as the mood took him: while Zoe, without realising it, was slowly and steadily going round in circles, finishing up pretty well at the same spot where she had begun.

Oh, yes – it would have been highly entertaining to anyone with an overall view of the proceedings.

And strangely enough – there was just such an observer, sitting comfortable in the Control Centre, watching all that took place, displayed on a gallery of television screens.

'Well done, well done,' he chuckled gently, as he monitored three different cameras – one trained on Zoe, one on Jamie, and one on the Doctor himself.

If the Doctor could have heard him, he would have recognised that soft-spoken, yet menacing voice: for it was the same voice which had persuaded him to leave the TARDIS in the first place.

Now he sat alone, in the Control Centre, at the heart of the Citadel – the nerve-centre from which he ruled this entire domain: and he was known to all those beneath him as 'the Master'.

Like that renegade member of the Doctor's own race, with whom he shared the same name, he seemed to be almost ominiscient: nothing happened in this strangely private universe without the Master knowing about it instantly; and nothing *could* occur unless he gave it his approval, and allowed it to take place.

'Well done,' he repeated, rubbing his hands gleefully. 'A very good beginning . . . Let us see how the story unfolds.'

Unaware that he was under surveillance, Jamie struggled on through the forest, trying to pick his way amongst the multitude of tree trunks.

It reminded him a little of days long, long ago – at home in the Highlands, when he and his friends had taken to the wild woodlands, at the time of the Rising of 1745. On the run from the English soldiers with their red coats and their muskets, they had lived rough for weeks on end, hiding out during the day and making forays across country by night.

He remembered nights as dark as this, dodging the enemy among the Scottish pine trees, in the small hours just before dawn . . . But this was somehow different.

He stood stock still, listening.

That was the difference. In the old times, he would have heard the night sounds of the forest – a waking bird twittering, the bark of a fox, the breathing of the living world about him . . . Perhaps too the cracking of a twig underfoot, or the distant rattle of gunfire.

Here there was nothing but silence: an unnatural, lifeless silence.

And then, as he stood listening, he heard a voice far away calling his name.

'Jamie! Jamie – Doctor – where are you?'

She was a long way off, but he recognised her immediately.

'Zoe!' he shouted back, cupping his hands to his mouth: 'I'm over here – where are you?'

He stumbled on, hoping he was going the right way – and the voice came again: 'Jamie – where are you?'

It was fainter than before, and now the sound echoed eerily, with overlapping reverberations from all sides: he hesitated, confused.

'Zoe? Keep calling, till I find you!'

Then he plunged ahead once more, putting on speed as he picked out a shadowy figure – a dark shape against a darker background.

'Zoe – is that you?'

But the words froze on his lips: he felt his heart miss a beat, as he took another step forward, and recognised the cut of an eighteenth-century uniform . . . Was he back in his own time after all?,

For the stranger was dressed like an English Redcoat, in a tall military shako like an upturned bucket, with scarlet jacket and buckskin breeches . . . His old enemy.

Hearing Jamie's voice, the soldier turned, raising his musket threateningly. Instinctively, Jamie pulled out the sheath knife which he carried at all times. If he was to be massacred in cold blood, he could at least defend himself. The soldier clicked the flintlock, about to fire.

'Shoot me down like a dog, would you?' Jamie roared, his fighting blood aroused. 'Well, a McCrimmon never died without a struggle yet! *Creag an tuire!*'

With the old Gaelic warcry on his lips he threw himself on his foe – and at the same instant, the Redcoat pulled the trigger.

There was a deafening explosion, and a cloud of white, pungent smoke. When the fumes died away, the English soldier had vanished . . . Jamie was alone: but totally changed.

He stood there, exactly as he had been at the instant when the musket was fired, with his arm upraised and the knife in his hand – but he had undergone a horrible transformation.

He was stiff and motionless, translated into two dimensions, like a cardboard cutout. It was as if Jamie had suddenly ceased to be Jamie McCrimmon, and in his place was a black-and-white illustration – a lifelike drawing from the pages of a book.

At the same time, a little way off among the soaring tree trunks, Zoe was still trying to find Jamie. She was sure she had heard him calling out to her, not long ago, but then there had been a bang – and since then, nothing at all.

'Jamie . . . I'm here!' she repeated desperately, trying to

project her voice as far as possible. 'Are you there? Where are you?'

She hurried on, terrified that she would lose him again. To be so near and yet so far from help – it was almost too much to bear.

As she dodged round one of the mighty tree trunks, her skirt was snagged on a gnarled twig, and she twitched it away irritably. Then she stopped.

Her skirt? But she never wore skirts . . .

She looked down at herself and caught her breath. For the silver jumpsuit had gone, and in its place was a long dress of pale blue, with a silk sash at her waist, and a full skirt, puffed out by stiff under-petticoats. She was wearing high-buttoned boots and – when she put her hand to her head she found a band of ribbon tying back her long hair.

Countless millions of children on twentieth-century Earth would have known her at once: but in the City where Zoe was born and brought up, no-one had ever heard of Alice in Wonderland.

This was why when she saw a giant mushroom with a caterpillar on top of it, half-hidden in the shadows, she did not feel any sense of recognition. A moment later, there was a flash of white fur and a flustered rabbit scuttered by.

Zoe blinked. Could the white rabbit really have been consulting a pocket-watch? Nonsense – she must be imagining things. Besides, this half-light was very deceptive: it played tricks with your eyes.

If only she had been familiar with the ways of Wonderland, she might have been better prepared for the trap that lay ahead.

She turned the corner of a winding path, and was brought to a standstill, for a high brick wall faced her – a wall with a door in it. But the door was firmly shut, and the wall seemed to go on for ever; there was no getting round it. She turned to retrace her steps – and found another wall right behind her. She looked right and left, and realised with a sickening feeling of doom that she had been boxed in, caught between four walls which hadn't been there a moment earlier.

'Doctor!' she cried in sudden panic. 'Help me – where are you? . . . *Help*!'

But her voice bounced back at her from these four blank walls. No-one could hear her now: she was shut in and imprisoned.

She returned automatically to the first wall, because that at least had a door in it and seemed to promise a way of escape. As she moved towards it, the door opened as if to welcome her, swinging back on rusty hinges with a high-pitched squeak that set her teeth on edge. But still – she couldn't retreat now. She could only go on.

Through the door she could see nothing but darkness, and she hesitated for a moment; then took her courage in both hands and told herself: 'Perhaps it won't be so gloomy once my eyes get used to it . . . And anyway, I'm not afraid of the dark!'

So she stepped bravely through the doorway – and at once the floor opened up beneath her feet, and she gave a cry of terror as she fell – down . . . down . . . down . . . Would the fall never come to an end?

Poor Zoe! How could she know that it was only a rabbit hole?

Somewhere in the Citadel, the Master hugged himself with delight: 'Dear Lewis Carroll,' he murmured. 'Always so reliable . . . '

He checked the bank of monitor screens once more: there was Zoe, tumbling down Alice's rabbit hole – there was Jamie, frozen into a storybook illustration – but the third screen was unaccountably blank.

The Doctor had disappeared.

The Master thumped his clenched fist on the desk in front of him, and barked out an order, his usually mild voice suddenly harsh and impatient: 'Where is the Doctor? Look around – he must be here somewhere . . . Find him . . . Search – all of you – *search*!'

Quickly he pressed several buttons, punching up more and more pictures on the rows of screens before him – but although they gave him many different views of the forest mazes, there was no sign of the Doctor.

'I see,' he said at last, trying to control his anger. 'He has eluded us for the moment, so he is not yet completely under my control . . . Very well – perhaps it is better this way . . . But keep searching – he must be found!'

Daylight was breaking through at last: the first long, level rays of sunlight penetrated the forest – like aisles of a cathedral, and the Doctor began to feel a little more optimistic. He might be fighting an unknown and invisible enemy, but at least he was no longer playing Blind Man's Bluff.

If only he knew where the others had got to . . .

He called out again: 'Zoe? Jamie? Is there anybody there?'

From far, far away, he thought he could just detect a cry in response: but the sounds were so distant, it was hard to be sure. Was it really his two young companions, or simply a flirting echo of his own words, reverberating through the trees?

'Zoe . . . Jamie . . . *Doctor* . . .'

He held his breath: that was no echo. He was about to shout again, louder than ever, but another sound reached him, from a different direction. It was the tramp of marching feet, and they were coming closer and closer.

The hair prickled at the back of his neck: he sensed danger. From the sound of that approaching army, he knew that these were not friends, but foes . . . He had to take cover.

'Very fortunate that these trees are so curiously shaped,' he muttered to himself. 'That one over there – its trunk is hollowed out, almost like a sentry box. If I slip inside, I'll be very well hidden.'

No sooner said than done. He dived inside the sheltering tree trunk, and waited tensely for the enemy to arrive.

The sound of marching feet was getting louder at every moment: and he risked peering out, very cautiously, to catch a glimpse of his opponents.

They were heading towards him, silhouetted against the dazzle of the early morning sunlight, so he could not see them clearly: from the outline of their uniform, they seemed to be old-fashioned British soldiery. They looked not unlike the Redcoat trooper Jamie had encountered earlier, with the same high military shakos – but these soldiers carried no muskets; and there was one other, vital difference.

At the front of each helmet, there was a round compound lens of ribbed glass, with a beam of light shining from it, like a miniature searchlight.

The Doctor had seen those strange head lamps before: the White Robots had carried something very similar. So, these invading troops must be another task force within the same regiment – but under whose orders, he wondered.

And, as he saw the line of soldiers march past his hiding place, with their heads turning left and right, and the rays of light from their helmet lamps, criss-crossing and probing into every dark corner, he shrank back into his hiding-place, and wondered what these strange devices were for.

If he had been with the Master, in his control centre, high up in the Citadel, he would have known at once. Each 'lamp' was serving a double function – to throw a beam of light, but also to record whatever it 'saw' and transmit an image back to the banks of monitor screens.

The Master studied the various screens intently: he saw a dozen pictures of tree trunks sliding by, from a dozen different angles – but of the Doctor there was still no sign.

'He can't be far away,' he announced. 'Continue on your present course – search all areas . . . These are your orders – he must be found!'

The Doctor waited, with bated breath, until the last sounds of marching feet died away, and then decided it was safe to come out of hiding.

He emerged cautiously from the tree trunk, about to set off once more – when a new and unfamiliar voice made him almost jump out of his skin.

'*Heckinah degul*!' The words were unfamiliar, but their meaning was clear enough. '*Tolgo phonae*!'

The Doctor put his hands above his head immediately.

The stranger was only a few paces away: he was dressed in eighteenth-century costume, with his hair scraped back into a short pigtail, and tied with a velvet knot. He wore a full-skirted coat reaching to his knees, unbuttoned shirt and breeches, and a three-cornered hat on his head. And he carried a small flintlock pistol, which he pointed directly at the Doctor's heart.

The Doctor licked his lips, and said nervously, 'I beg your pardon – I didn't quite catch . . . ?'

The stranger frowned, and took a step towards him, menacingly.

'*Langro dehul san* . . . ?'

The Doctor considered himself to be reasonably fluent in foreign tongues, but these words were Double Dutch to him. He shook his head with a polite but regretful smile, and asked: '*Parlez-vous français*?'

The stranger appeared to be trying out alternative languages, and persevered. '*Grildig? Splacknuck*?'

The Doctor tried again: 'Do you speak English by any chance?'

A broad smile broke over the man's face: and the Doctor felt suddenly reassured. Whoever this man might be, he had a frank, humorous expression; he did not appear to be a villain. And – wonder of wonders – he spoke English, even if his phraseology was a little old-fashioned.

'Sir! My birth was of honest parents, in an island called England!'

'Good gracious me – why didn't you say so before?' said the Doctor.

'I spoke in as many languages as I had the least smattering of – lingua franca, high and low Dutch – '

'Ah, Double Dutch – I thought as much – well, let's start all over again, shall we? May I ask when you were last in England?'

The stranger knitted his brows with the effort to

47

remember: 'We set sail from Bristol on May the Fourth, 1699.'

'We?'

'What became of my companions, I cannot tell; they were all lost.'

The Doctor sighed sympathetically: 'I know how you feel, my dear chap . . . You and I are in the same boat.'

The stranger's face lit up. 'You have a stout ship?' he asked.

He came eagerly up to the Doctor, still holding the pistol, although he appeared to have forgotten it. The Doctor turned the muzzle away with one finger, and exclaimed: 'Do put that pop-gun away, there's a good fellow – do you mind? It rather unsettles me.'

The stranger, obligingly slipped it into a side-pocket of his coat, as the Doctor continued: 'What I mean is – I've lost my companions as well; two of them – a boy and a girl – Jamie and Zoe . . . I suppose you haven't come across them in your travels, by any chance?'

'Alas, no.' The stranger shook his head.

'No. Well, I've got to find them. Perhaps you'd care to come along and help me search, if you know your way around these parts?'

The stranger's face changed; it was as if a shadow had fallen across his lively eyes, and they now appeared dark and brooding. Then: 'It is not permitted,' he said flatly.

'Not permitted? Who says so?'

'The Master.'

The Doctor scratched his head. 'Who's he when he's at home? The Master of what? Master of where? Who is he?'

The stranger continued in the same monotone: 'He has articles of impeachment against you, for treason and other capital crimes.'

'Treason? Oh, really! How can I be a traitor when I don't even know where I am or what I'm doing here? Where *am* I, as a matter of interest? What is the name of this extra-ordinary place?'

'I cannot tell.'

'Well, that makes two of us. So, you won't help me – is that what you're saying?'

'Sir, if you assure me you are no traitor – perhaps I may accompany you upon some later occasion . . . But for now – I will leave to your prudence what measures you will take . . . And to avoid suspicion, I must immediately retire, in as private a manner as I came.'

With these words, the stranger swept off his tricorne hat, and made a very civil bow. Then he stepped back and moved behind a tree, out of sight.

The Doctor began to protest: 'Hey – don't run away when I'm talking to you – there are lots more questions I want to ask. Come back here, my dear chap – '

He followed in his footsteps, circling the tree. But there was no-one there. The empty paths stretched out in all directions, but there was no sign of the stranger. He had disappeared into thin air.

The Doctor rubbed his eyes: 'A hallucination, perhaps? Am I dreaming things? Was there anyone here at all? Oh, dear – how very tiresome.'

There was nothing for it but to continue with his quest.

By now, the Master was becoming more than a little impatient.

The Scottish boy and the Alice in Wonderland girl had been satisfactorily disposed of in their different ways: but what had become of the Doctor?

He drummed his fingers on the desk irritably, and then made another announcement to the minions who obeyed his command.

'We can't waste any more time – do you hear? You've let me down badly – all of you. The Doctor is still at large, and he must be found. If not by the usual methods – then I shall have to try something else . . . Something a little more subtle.'

He rubbed his chin thoughtfully.

'Let me see – a real puzzle, this time – something worthy of the good Doctor's brilliant mind . . . First, we must drive him out of hiding, and then put him on his mettle. We need to employ our most fiendish inquisitors . . . The riddlers, the testers, the teasers and tormentors . . . Get to work, all of you - you know what must be done. Go out and play games with him!'

A gleam of excitement lit up the Master's moist blue eyes. This was going to be a real battle of wits.

The inquisitors set about their task at once: and they tackled it far more cleverly than the regimented soldiery, who could only obey direct commands. This second wave of shock-troops represented a very different power - the Intelligence Corps.

As the Master had stated, the Doctor could not be far away; so they began to hunt the area systematically, dividing it up between them, working down each forest path in turn, searching every tree, every secluded corner, every possible hiding place, like beaters flushing out game before a shoot.

As they proceeded to put the Master's scheme into operation, the Doctor himself - blissfully unaware that the hunt was up - slogged on through the tree trunks, still looking for Jamie and Zoe.

He was getting weary now. He had been on the move for a considerable time, and his legs were tired and aching - but he would not give up.

The weather was changing too; the bright early sunlight had clouded over, and now a kind of haze shrouded the forest. Wisps of fog hung motionless among the tall trees, and the Doctor shivered a little. He hoped with all his heart that the mist wouldn't become any thicker: his quest was bad enough without that - in thick fog it would be quite impossible.

'Zoe - Jamie - ' he called, as he had been calling at intervals all the morning.

This time he heard a reply, loud and clear, and very close at hand.

'Cooeee!' called a girl's voice. 'Count up to a hundred and we'll find you!'

A boy's voice chimed in: 'Coming – ready or not!'

The Doctor looked around in bewilderment. It didn't sound quite like Zoe and Jamie, but at least it appeared that help was at hand. He began to do as he was told, counting rapidly aloud: 'One, two, three, four, five, six, seven . . . '

He had only got as far as twenty-three when they found him.

First a little girl stepped out of the mist . . . She was dressed in a pinafore dress that reached below her knees, and wore a big floppy sunhat. She was followed almost immediately by another girl, a little older, wheeling a doll's perambulator – and then three boys appeared from nowhere: one in a schoolcap and blazer, another in white flannels, who carried a cricket bat, and the third in a tweed Norfolk jacket and knickerbockers. They all looked as if they had stepped out of the pages of a juvenile story by E. Nesbit or Kenneth Grahame.

The Doctor smiled as he welcomed them: he felt reassured at once – they looked so cosily familiar, and summoned up remembrances of golden summer days and childhoods long ago.

'Well, well!' he exclaimed cheerfully. 'This is a pleasant surprise – how do you do?'

But the children were not smiling. They stared at him silently, and moved in to surround him.

'We've caught you,' said the eldest girl, solemnly. 'Now you're "he" . . . But you can't run off and hide again, you have to answer our questions first.'

The Doctor looked from one accusing gaze to another. Perhaps they were not quite as harmless as he had first supposed.

'Questions?' he repeated. 'What questions?'

The riddles came at him from all sides, delivered at machine-gun speed.

'Why did the chicken cross the road?' – 'Where was Moses when the light went out?' – 'How many beans make five?' – 'How long is a piece of string?'

The Doctor tried to answer as best he could, but they all

kept talking at once, and he couldn't remember half the answers – it was all extremely confusing.

'Which is correct – the yolk of an egg *is* white, or the yolk of an egg *are* white?'

'Are – is – ' the Doctor stammered, then corrected himself, in the nick of time. 'No, no – of course not, it's a catch – the yolk of an egg *are* yellow!'

Still the riddles continued: 'Adam and Eve and Pinch-Me went down to the river to bathe; Adam and Eve got drowned – so who do you think was saved?'

'The Doctor began: 'Pinch-Me, obviously, but – '

Instantly they fell upon him, squealing gleefully and pinching him all over, with cruel, pointed fingers.

'Ouch – stop – don't do that – !' The Doctor protested. 'I've had quite enough riddles, thank you – now it's time for me to ask you some questions. First and foremost, what are your names, and where have you – '

But they weren't even listening. The boy with the cricket bat raised it like a weapon – and suddenly it was no longer a wooden bat, but a wickedly sharp sword of polished steel, and the swordpoint was at the Doctor's throat.

'What can you make of a sword?' the boy demanded.

The Doctor gulped, trying to make sense of this nightmare examination.

'What? I don't understand – ' he gasped.

The other children joined in the attack: 'What *can* you make of it?'

'Rearrange it – think!'

'This is your last chance!'

The youngest girl spelled it out for him: 'S-W-O-R-D – rearrange!'

The Doctor thought desperately: it was clearly some kind of brainteaser – a rearrangement of letters – an anagram . . . If you rearranged the word SWORD you could make it spell – '*Words*!' he exclaimed triumphantly, feeling the blade below his chin.

The children cheered and clapped their hands: the boy threw the sword high into the air, and when it came down again, it had turned into a dictionary, which landed slap in the Doctor's outstretched hands . . . A book of words, of course: that's what it had all been about – rhymes and riddles and word play . . .

The eldest girl said politely: 'You have given the correct answer . . . You may well be suitable . . . I do hope so, for your sake.'

Then she stopped and listened: somewhere a bell was clanging.

'Hurry up,' said the cricketing boy. 'That means they're closing the park gates . . . Time to go home – time for tea.'

'Buttered toast and plum cake for tea today!' shouted the boy in knickerbockers. 'Come on, I'll race you!'

And they all ran off, shouting and laughing: their voices dying away into the distance, as the fog swallowed them up.

For it was getting thicker all the time. The Doctor began to walk once more, pondering what he had just heard.

'You may well be suitable' . . . Suitable? But for what?

The light was fading fast, and he had to put his hands out before him, to avoid bumping into the trees. Surely it couldn't be night-time already?

Straining his eyes, he peered through the gloom: was that one of the children, waiting for him just ahead? He pressed on, and his heart leaped as he recognised the familiar silhouette of a boy in a kilt . . .

'*Jamie!*' he cried joyfully. 'There you are – at last!'

By now it was so dark, he could hardly distinguish any details of Jamie's appearance, but he continued eagerly: 'I'm so glad to see you, my lad. Not that I can see you very clearly: do you suppose there's going to be a storm? What do you think?'

Oddly, Jamie made no reply. The Doctor turned to him, questioningly: 'Why don't you say something? What's wrong, Jamie?'

As he spoke, there was a crash of thunder, followed almost instantly by a startling flash of lightning.

For a brief moment, the forest was lit up brilliantly, and

53

the Doctor could see every detail. He felt a chill of sheer horror, which gripped his heart like an icy hand.

Now he knew why Jamie was dumb. He could not speak, or see, for he had no features at all. Where eyes, nose and mouth should have been, was a smooth blank oval . . .

Jamie had no face.

4

Dangerous Games

It was one of the most terrifying moments the Doctor had ever known.

Here was his young friend – safe and sound in every particular, but a hideous trick had been played on him. What fiendish intelligence could have devised such a punishment – and *why*?

The Doctor's mind raced; he had to stay calm, and try to find some way to put things right . . . To turn this zombie-like figure into Jamie once again.

At least the storm clouds appeared to be lifting; the sky was growing lighter. A thin ray of watery sun filtered through the forest glade, and illuminated a strange object which had been hidden in the shadows until now. The Doctor stared at it: it appeared to be an old-fashioned school blackboard, propped up on an easel . . . But there were no chalked inscriptions upon it.

Instead, he found himself gazing at assorted scraps of old photographs – some in colour, some black-and-white – details cut out of various pictures . . . Each of them contained a section of a face – some eyes here, a nose there, a selection of mouths, chins, cheekbones . . .

'So that's it,' the Doctor muttered to himself. 'Another

test, obviously. I have to select the correct features and put them together to make up Jamie's face! Very well - so be it.'

He set to work as quickly as possible: 'Eyes - let me see, what colour are Jamie's eyes? Hazel, I think - a brownish-green . . . And that's definitely the lad's cheeky nose - I'd recognise it anywhere!'

He soon collected a handful of photographic scraps, shuffling them into position on the blackboard in an attempt to recreate Jamie's familiar image. But then he got distracted at a crucial moment.

The misty clouds continued to roll back, and sunlight touched first one and then another area of the forest that until now had been shrouded in darkness. And in each area a strange artifact stood revealed - a bizarre collection of items.

The Doctor stared at them . . . An old-fashioned steel safe, with a wheel-shaped combination lock . . . A gigantic cut-out of an upraised hand, with a letter scrawled upon its palm . . . And - most unlikely of all - a traditional wishing well, with a thatched roof, and a wooden bucket.

The Doctor examined each of these extraordinary objects with great care: he tried the door of the safe, but it remained obstinately locked. He peered into the well, hoping to discover the truth, - for wasn't truth to be found at the bottom of a well, according to the ancient legend? But all he saw was the reflection of his own puzzled face staring back at him, far below.

'Of course - this is a wishing well . . . ' The Doctor racked his brains. 'I wish - I wish - oh, dear me, I wish I believed in wishing wells . . . '

From somewhere up above him, he thought he heard a ghostly chuckle of laughter, and looked up in alarm - but he could see nothing there.

Nothing, that is, except the last traces of mist, still hanging about the tree tops - and, before his astonished gaze, two faint, floating letters half-shrouded in the mist. An 'm' and a 't', both with a diagonal stroke through them, as if they had been crossed out.

'Wait a bit . . . I've seen something like that, somewhere before,' he said to himself.

Then he looked again at the cut-out hand, which also had a letter written upon it - the letter 'h' - and saw that this too had been crossed out and cancelled.

'It's very puzzling,' he mused - and suddenly slapped his forehead. 'Ye Gods, I need my brains taken out and buttered - I must be losing my grip. A puzzle! Of course - that's what it is - a picture puzzle - a rebus.'

It was the sort of thing one sometimes finds in children's comics or annuals; a sentence made up of pictures, where each picture represents a word, if one can interpret them correctly.

Hopefully, the Doctor began to put the images into the correct order: first Jamie - poor, faceless Jamie . . . Then the misty letters, the safe, the hand, the wishing well.

But the 'm' and 't' had been blotted out from the mist - so 'mist' became 'is' . . . Just as 'hand' without the 'h' became 'and'.

At once the whole thing fell into place.

'*Jamie . . . Is . . . Safe . . . And . . . Well.*'

As the Doctor repeated the five words aloud, there was one final clap of thunder, and a flash of lighting: and Jamie came to life again.

'Hey, Doctor!' he exclaimed joyfully, grabbing the Doctor's hand and shaking it vigorously. 'I'm certainly glad to see you - I thought for a while I'd lost you for good!'

The Doctor withdrew his hand, confused and ill-at-ease. For the voice was Jamie's voice - he was in no doubt about that - but the face was somehow unrecognisable. Were those really Jamie's eyes? Was his mouth quite so wide - or his chin so pointed?

Before he could stop himself he blurted out in dismay: 'I must have got it wrong. You're not Jamie!'

The Scottish boy grinned: but it was a stranger's grin. 'What are ye on about now?'

'Well - you - your face - it - it's different . . . '

'How d'ye mean - different?'

The Doctor fumbled in his pocket and brought out a small hand-mirror, which he passed over.

'See for yourself.'

Jamie looked at his unfamiliar reflection – and recoiled: 'That's no my face – I've never seen it before in my life.'

'Maybe not,' sighed the Doctor, 'but it seems to be the one you're stuck with at present – so we'll both have to get used to it.'

'But why? How did it happen?'

'All I can tell you is that it's a particularly nasty trick on the part of the person who brought us here,' replied the Doctor – and he looked up at the sky, accusingly.

This time there was no question about it: he heard a far-off shout of gleeful, malicious laughter . . . The Master – whoever he might be – was obviously most amused at this turn of events.

From now on, the Doctor realised, he could no longer trust anything that might happen – or that might seem to be happening. Everything was a minefield of tests and traps and practical jokes: and appearances were always deceptive.

'How do I know you are Jamie?' he enquired bitterly. 'How do I know you're not another illusion sent to confuse me still further?'

'Of course I'm Jamie!' snorted the boy, indignantly. 'I told you so – I'm still *me* even if I can't recognise myself!'

'But how do I know I can believe you?' the Doctor persisted. 'Can you prove to me that you're Jamie McCrimmon? Where have you come from? How did you get here?'

Jamie scratched his head, and tried to remember.

'It's hard to say . . . It's all a wee bit hazy . . . The last thing I really remember clearly is a dream I had.'

'A dream?'

'Aye – I was telling you about it when I woke up, don't you remember? We were in the TARDIS: I'd been snatching forty winks, and in my dream there was this beautiful white unicorn . . . Beautiful – but frightening – because the dream turned into a nightmare. The unicorn

57

lowered its head and began to charge at me – pointing its horn towards me as if it would run me through . . . '

The Doctor's brow cleared: and he smiled with relief.

'Yes – now you mention it, I *do* remember you telling me about that dream. But what happened next?'

'Well, there was this unicorn – head down, ready for the kill – and then everything went crazy, and I was off.'

'Off? Off where? Where have you been?'

'In a fog . . . I mean *really* in a fog. Ever since the TARDIS broke up.'

The Doctor repeated his words automatically: 'Ever since the TARDIS broke up – ' and suddenly realised what he was saying. 'It did *what*?'

He grabbed Jamie's arms, and demanded: 'What are you telling me? What's happened to the TARDIS?'

'It broke up – fell to bits – I thought you knew that . . . We all flew off into space – and then somehow we finished up here. You, me and – ' He hesitated, looking around, then said in a small voice: 'And Zoe . . . ? Where is she?'

The Doctor looked very grave. 'I wish I knew. I suspect she's been caught up in some sort of trap – just as we have.'

'A trap? What sort of trap?' He stared at the towering tree trunks that surrounded them. 'Where exactly are we, anyway?'

'I can't tell you, I'm afraid. All I can tell you is that – wherever we are – we were expected. There's been quite a welcoming committee prepared to meet us.'

Jamie scratched his head, completely bewildered.

'How do you mean?'

'We were brought here as part of a plan, by someone who calls himself the Master, apparently. But what or where he is Master of, I have yet to discover. The only thing I know for sure is that he enjoys setting puzzles – brainteasers – tricks and riddles.'

'Riddles?' The boy still looked blank. 'I don't under-stand.'

'You will, Jamie – you will.'

And as if to illustrate this point, they were interrupted by a plaintive call for help – a muffled voice, that seemed to be coming from inside a prison: '*Doctor – Jamie – help me!*'

Jamie's head snapped up instantly: 'There she is – that's Zoe!'

The Doctor shouted as loudly as he could: 'Yes, Zoe – we hear you – where are you?'

The reply came in the same indistinct tone: 'I'm trapped – I can't get out – please help me!'

Jamie began to run towards the source of the sound, exclaiming: 'I think she's over here somewhere!'

The Doctor set off at a jog trot after him, both of them weaving their way along the winding paths that snaked through the tall trees. As the Doctor had realised earlier, the strange formation of closely-planted trees made an excellent hiding place – but when you were trying to find someone lost in that maze, it presented problems.

They searched here and there, down long alleys that led off into darkness, and time and again came up short against a huge tree trunk blocking their path. Only Zoe's encouraging cries spurred them on.

It was like one of those tantalising nursery games of 'Hunt the Thimble'; as Zoe's voice got louder or fainter, they felt the trail growing 'hot' or 'cold'.

Then, quite suddenly, they turned a corner, and knew they were at their journey's end.

They had reached an old oak door set in a blank wall: a heavy door, studded with bolts, under a gothic arch. And from the other side of the door, Zoe's voice called desperately: 'I can't get out . . . Help me – please!'

Jamie put his shoulder to the timbers and tried to shove – but it was impossible: the door wouldn't budge an inch.

'There's no handle,' he grumbled, searching for some way to tackle it. 'No sign of a lock either.'

The Doctor ran his fingertips over the surface of the wood, and said, 'It's hardly surprising – when you consider that this isn't even a real door. Don't you see? It's another illusion – a wall, with a door painted on to it.'

59

Jamie scratched at it with his fingernails. The Doctor was right. It was not wood, but solid, unyielding stone. 'But that's crazy!' he exploded. 'How can anyone get through a door that isn't a door?'

His words rang a bell somewhere at the back of the Doctor's mind . . . A door that wasn't a door . . .

'Give me a moment to think – ' he muttered, massaging his temples, as if he were trying to press his brain on to greater efforts. 'I must *think* . . . '

'What's the good of thinking?' Jamie stormed impatiently. 'What we want is a battering ram – maybe if we could cut down one of those trees – '

But the Doctor wasn't listening. 'When is a door not a door?' he asked, with a chuckle.

'Och – this is no time for riddles – '

'That's where you're wrong! I told you – this *is* a time and a place for riddles! When is a door not a door? When it's ajar!'

As he answered the riddle the solid-looking door melted away into mist, and through it they saw Zoe – her dark hair dishevelled, her silver jumpsuit curiously distorted – trapped inside a huge, transparent jar, and beating her fists against the glass.

Jamie began to laugh: – he couldn't help it for she really did look rather comical. 'At least that's kept you out of mischief for a while!' he commented.

'Oh, you – !' Zoe was crosser than ever. 'Get me out of here!'

It didn't take long. The Doctor gave Jamie a leg-up and he climbed to the top of the jar, then leaned over and stretched down, holding out his hands to Zoe.

She clutched at him, and he hauled her up. A moment later, they had both scrambled down again, and she was free.

'Oh – thank goodness!' she panted. 'I began to think I was never going to get out of there.'

She dusted herself down, and then took a closer look at her rescuer – and her face changed. 'Just a minute – you're not Jamie. Who are you?'

He groaned: 'Don't you start – I've had enough trouble from the Doctor already . . . I tell you I'm Jamie McCrimmon – I'm me!'

Zoe turned to the Doctor for confirmation. 'But why does he look so different?' she asked.

The Doctor examined his fingernails uncomfortably, and cleared his throat: 'Uh – er – a slight technical hitch, my dear . . . I'll explain later. First of all, I think we should get out of this forest, don't you?'

Jamie nodded vehemently: 'The sooner the better – this place gives me the shivers . . . Come on – I'll lead the way.'

He set off among the trees at a brisk pace, and the others followed a little more slowly. Zoe clutched at the Doctor's sleeve and whispered: 'Is that *really* Jamie? Are you quite sure?'

The Doctor said sadly· 'Oh, yes, it really is . . . He's just – changed a little – that's all.'

'But he couldn't have! It's impossible!'

'I think, Zoe, that we are now in a place where nothing is impossible. Come on – we don't want to lose him again.'

They trudged on and on through the forest, hoping to find a way out, but without any success. The tall trees seemed to stretch on into the distance for mile after mile – and at last Zoe called a halt.

'I don't care what you say – I want to sit and rest for a while. I had to stand up inside that beastly jam jar, because there wasn't enough room to sit down – and my feet hurt!' She flopped down on the ground then and there, sitting with her back to one of the smooth tree trunks.

Jamie looked up at the treetops, squinting, and shielding his eyes against the light. 'It's very strange,' he said thoughtfully. 'I don't know if you've noticed it, Doctor, but these trees don't seem to have branches or leaves. They just stretch up into the sky, and then stop dead. If you could give me a leg up again, I might be able to climb up and see what's what.'

The Doctor agreed it was worth a try: 'You might be able to see a way out of the wood from the top . . . As things are down here, we can't see the wood for the trees – to coin a phrase.'

The Doctor braced himself against a tree trunk so that Jamie could use his clasped hands and shoulder as footholds – and the boy scrambled up the rest of the way.

Finally he called down triumphantly: 'I've done it – I've got to the top – ' And then his voice altered and he sounded quite awestruck. 'Doctor . . . You're never going to believe this.'

'Just at present, I think I'd believe almost anything,' responded the Doctor. 'Why – what is it? Can you see something?'

'Och, I can see all right . . . Do you know what this tree really is?'

'No – what?'

'It's a letter "B" – stretched out, twenty feet tall, with one flat side and two round ones . . . And the next tree is an "S" – and then there's an "O", hollow all the way down – and a "W" . . . All the trees are letters: we've been walking through a forest of words!'

The Doctor shut his eyes. 'Of course . . . This is a world of words – I should have realised it.'

Zoe called up: 'What do the words say?'

From his vantage point on the treetop, Jamie spelled them out with difficulty: 'Slow . . . but . . . sure . . . In . . . for . . . a . . . penny – '

'In for a pound – yes, all old sayings – proverbs.' The Doctor was no longer going to be surprised by anything.

'Look – before – you leap . . . ' Jamie continued, then: 'And they go on and on like that – but too far away – I can't read any more. Look out; I'm coming down.'

He slithered down the treetrunk again, landing lightly upon his feet.

'The important question is – did you see a way out?' Zoe asked.

'Not really – except it looked as if the trees thin out a bit, in this direction – ' He pointed to one side: and stopped short with a gasp. For, out of nowhere, they had been joined by a stranger – the gentleman in the three-cornered hat whom the Doctor had already met, earlier in the day.

Zoe gave a little cry of dismay, and the Doctor was quick to reassure her. 'Don't be alarmed, Zoe – this gentleman and I are old friends: he is a traveller too, just like ourselves.'

The stranger doffed his hat and made a low bow to Zoe, then acknowledged Jamie with a courteous salute. 'Your servant, ma'am . . . sir!'

The Doctor welcomed him warmly: 'So we meet again, my dear chap. Allow me to introduce my two companions – Zoe and Jamie. I've found them at last, you see.'

They all muttered greetings and shook hands, as the Doctor continued: 'You find us still hopelessly lost, however. We were just trying to find our way out of this forest.'

The traveller shook his head dubiously: 'This resolution, perhaps, may appear very bold and dangerous.'

Zoe broke in: 'But we've got to get away from here!'

'Haven't you ever tried to find a way of escaping from this place?' asked the Doctor.

'No,' said the man simply. 'I looked upon myself to be fully settled for life.'

Jamie persisted: 'But all these tests – the tricks and the riddles – don't they get on your nerves? What's the point of them?'

The stranger regarded him solemnly for a moment, then replied: 'In choosing persons for all employments, they have regard to great abilities. A course of study is required, to qualify any man for the service of his country.'

Zoe and Jamie exchanged glances: the stranger appeared to be friendly and forthcoming, yet his replies never seemed to answer their questions completely. Zoe tried again: 'But who's in charge here? Who's been setting all these traps?'

The man glanced over his shoulder and lowered his voice as he answered: 'The Master . . . '

'So you told me,' said the Doctor. 'And that clockwork army serves the Master as well, I take it?'

'Army?' The man repeated the word, puzzled. 'As to their military affairs – I know not what they meant.'

63

'But surely – you must have seen them – a whole troop of mechanical soldiers – '

The stranger only shook his head and repeated: 'I know not what they meant.'

And at that instant, they heard the sound of marching feet coming towards them. The Doctor reacted promptly: 'There they are. That's the noise they make – I've seen them before – they're coming this way!'

Zoe looked around fearfully: 'What do we do?'

'We hide – that's what! Quickly – you can both squeeze into the letter "C" – there's room for two. I'll make myself a sentry-box of the letter "J" . . . But hurry – they mustn't find us!'

No sooner said than done: they all took refuge in the giant letters – only the eighteenth-century traveller stayed where he was, quite unperturbed, as the Doctor asked: 'And you, sir? Aren't you going to take cover?'

He smiled, and replied confidently: 'The best expedient I could think on, was to keep guard.'

The Doctor accepted this: 'Splendid . . . If you are in no danger yourself, that sounds like an excellent scheme . . . Keep out of sight, Zoe!'

She stuck her head out of the encircling column of the letter 'C' long enough to say to their new-found ally: 'Don't give us away – whatever you do!'

And then they all three withdrew into their hiding places.

For a long time, nothing happened – except that the sound of marching feet grew steadily louder. The stranger hummed a little tune under his breath, and waited.

Then, at last, the army of tin soldiers came into sight: row upon row of mechanical figures advancing in formation. As they approached, Zoe, hidden within the hollow letter-tree, held her breath.

The man in the tricorne hat gazed out into the distance, past the columns of soldiers, without a sign of recognition. The troops stamped to attention, forming up around him, but he gave them neither a word nor a glance. Instead, he stretched his arms, flexing his muscles and yawned.

Then he turned to the three others in their hiding places, and said easily: 'I could not forbear smiling. What you have told me is mistaken . . . There was no Army here.'

This was all the indication the enemy troops needed. They moved in on the hollow trees, and caught the fugitives in the brilliant rays of their compound lenses.

Far away in the Citadel, the Master leant forward, on the edge of his seat, watching the monitor screens that carried pictures of the trapped victims. Now they shuffled out of their hiding-places, half-dazzled by the glaring lights that beat upon them from all sides . . . It was hopeless to try and escape now; they were totally encircled and outnumbered.

'At last!' breathed the Master, exulting in his moment of triumph. 'Now round them up, and march them away . . . You have your orders – you know what must be done.'

The soldiers moved in, closer still, and the three prisoners were forced to move forward and fall in line – resistance was impossible.

As they passed the eighteenth-century traveller, who still gazed into space, apparently lost in his own thoughts, Jamie could not help saying sarcastically: 'Well, thank you very much – you were a big help!'

The man stared at Jamie, not entirely understanding him, and Zoe added reproachfully: 'We trusted you! Why did you give us away to the soldiers?'

The stranger shook his head, completely baffled: 'The soldiers? . . . But as I said – there was no Army here.'

And he wandered off among the mechanical soldiers, avoiding them by inches, without looking to left or right. Jamie was about to shout some rude retort after him, but the Doctor intervened: 'Save your breath, lad . . . There's no point in arguing – don't you understand yet? As far as he is concerned, they don't exist. They don't live in *his* world – so he can't see them.'

The stranger turned, and raised his hat politely once again, saying: 'And now, sir – I must forbear troubling you any further. Having answered the only objection you raise against me, I here take a final leave of you all.'

He bowed, and strode away among the trees, still whistling his little tune. Zoe clenched her fists: 'Oh, he makes me so angry – how can anyone be so – *detached*? Who does he think he is?'

The Doctor gave a faint, sympathetic smile: 'He knows who he is . . . And, so, I fancy, do I.' Then, as his two young companions were about to shower him with questions, he cut in: 'But we'll discuss these fascinating matters some other time. I think we have more immediate problems on hand – the soldiery seem to want us to go in the opposite direction.'

Sure enough, the mechanical army were on the move again, urging the prisoners onward with relentless steps.

Zoe found herself being herded forward, and suddenly exclaimed: 'Doctor . . . Just look at these soldiers – am I mad, or do they seem to be – well – *toy* soldiers?'

She pointed to the guards who surrounded them: and indeed, each soldier had a large wind-up key sticking out from the middle of his shoulderblades. They marched on automatically – left, right, left, right – their faces blank and expressionless, each with a round dab of crimson paint on his cheekbones, and a black moustache outlined under his nose . . . A victorious army of toy soldiers.

'Toys . . . Yes, my dear,' agreed the Doctor. 'Just like everything else in this world of imagination – tricks and riddles, toys and games . . . '

'Is that all they are? Just games?' Jamie repeated in amazement. 'Well, then, we've got nothing to be scared of – '

'I wouldn't be too sure about that,' the Doctor warned him, as the nursery troops hustled them away. 'They may not be real, but they're not exactly harmless . . . The games they play are dangerous games.'

At his Control Centre, the Master heard these words, and rubbed his hands in happy anticipation.

'Well done – well done,' he whispered. 'Now the real

battle of wits can begin . . . This is one game that must be played to the finish!'

The three prisoners were marched on relentlessly for what seemed to be a long time. They left the forest of words at last and emerged on to a vast, barren plain which stretched away on all sides – as far as the horizon. A shining black floor mirrored a shining black sky: apart from that, there was nothing to be seen. Then with one accord, the troops suddenly halted, and began to shift into new formation, wheeling left and right until they formed a hollow square.

Zoe, Jamie and the Doctor found themselves surrounded, and Zoe turned to the Doctor fearfully: 'What's happening? What are they going to do with us?'

She caught her breath – for the answer came, not from the Doctor, but from a disembodied voice high above them: '*You have to face the firing squad – unless you give the correct password.*'

She looked in all directions – whitefaced. 'Who was that? Who said that?'

The Doctor tried to speak calmly: 'The Master, I presume. But don't let it upset you – it's only another of his little games.'

'*A dangerous game I think you said, my dear Doctor?*' The Voice echoed from side to side of the vast empty plain. '*Yes – dangerous indeed . . . Unless you can provide the password.*'

Even as the Voice spoke, the front rank of troops took up their firing position. Each soldier dropped on to one knee, and levelled a musket.

'The password? What's he blethering about?' demanded Jamie, trying to sound more nonchalant than he really felt.

'*Two across and two down – Begin at the Beginning,*' said the Master's voice, mockingly. '*Four, four, one and four.*'

'He's off his head!' said Jamie, under his breath. 'There's no sense in any of this . . . He's talking in riddles again.'

'Riddles? No, not this time . . . Puzzles,' said the Doctor. 'Of course they were invented since your time, Jamie – you couldn't be expected to recognise a crossword puzzle clue.'

'A what?'

'A crossword puzzle.' The Doctor pointed to their feet. 'All we have to do is fill in the square.'

There, on the ground, was an empty grid of black and white squares: two up and two down . . . Four, four, one and four.

'I don't know what you're on about – what do we put on the squares?' Jamie asked.

'The letters that make up a four-word answer . . . And the clue is ''Begin at the Beginning'' . . . Four words that begin something,' the Doctor tried to explain.

Zoe looked up, and shivered: 'It's getting cold . . . This weather never stays the same for two minutes together . . . If we're not getting fog or thunder and lightning, we're going to be frozen to death. Look – it's starting to snow.'

As she spoke, the first flakes began to fall: huge white snowflakes – but very regular in shape – and each one had a letter of the alphabet marked upon it.

'Quick – catch them!' exclaimed the Doctor. 'Catch a falling letter – scoop up as many as you can – we may need them all!'

The snowstorm of letters came down thick and fast, and they did their best to grab them as they fluttered through the air. It was impossible to catch them all, and the ones that slipped through their fingers melted and vanished like real snowflakes as they met the floor.

But by the time the little wintry flurry was over, they had several handfuls of letters between them, and the Doctor read them out . . . Two 'O's, two 'N's, two 'F's – and a selection of single letters: C, U, P, A, T, I and M . . . Thirteen letters in all.

'Enough to make up three words of four letters and a one-letter word,' the Doctor concluded. 'It's an anagram – rearrange the letters, and you get – let me see – what does it spell? . . . ''*Once Upon A Time*'' . . .'

There was a sudden, short, sharp noise, and Zoe flinched, expecting a hail of bullets from the firing-squad. But it was only the noise of the robot army stamping to attention. They did a smart about-turn, and then marched off into the darkness, leaving the three travellers alone in the middle of the empty plain.

'That must have been what they wanted - the password . . .' Jamie breathed a sigh of relief.

'I think so . . . "Begin at the Beginning" - that's how all the best stories begin - "Once Upon A Time",' agreed the Doctor. 'We've stumbled across the password - the password to a world of fiction, where dreams and stories all come true.'

'But - if we've got the password - that means we're safe, doesn't it?' asked Zoe. 'It means we're free to go - ' She broke off, listening. 'What was that noise?'

It was a drumming: a kind of throbbing that grew louder and louder.

Jamie looked about him, uneasily, and said: 'I have an idea I've heard it before somewhere . . . In fact - I've got a funny feeling I've been here before . . . But I couldn't have - could I?'

The Doctor put a hand on his shoulder. 'Ssh! listen . . . It sounds like a horse galloping.'

Zoe chimed in: 'It's getting nearer - it's coming this way . . . Look - there it is - a white horse!'

Jamie followed the line of her outstretched hand: and then he stood transfixed, his face turning deathly pale. 'It's no horse,' he said huskily. 'D'you no see its one white horn - as sharp as a dagger?'

'A unicorn!' gasped Zoe.

'My dream . . . ' whispered Jamie. 'Like you said - my dream's come true . . . '

Zoe pulled at his arm: 'Quick - run for it - while we've still got a chance!'

'We have no chance at all,' said Jamie, as if he were under a spell. 'It's my nightmare again - only this time I can't wake up.'

The unicorn galloped straight towards them, and the noise of its hoofbeats was deafening as it lowered its head, and charged - ready for the kill.

5

Into the Labyrinth

The milk-white unicorn was a vision of beauty: moving with easy, liquid grace, its powerful muscles rippling under a satin skin. In the centre of its forehead, the single horn of polished ivory gleamed with a lustrous glow . . .

And it was pointing straight at Jamie's heart.

Beauty and terror combined to root him to the spot: he was powerless to run away. Zoe screamed at him to save himself, and tried to drag him bodily out of the path of the galloping animal: 'Run – get away – there's still time!'

But Jamie refused to budge, only shaking his head and saying: 'No . . . There's no time at all . . . I haven't got a chance.'

He never took his eyes off the unicorn as it raced nearer and nearer; he seemed to be almost hypnotised by it. He continued in the same flat monotone: 'Don't you see? It's my dream all over again.'

Zoe shook him desperately: 'It's *not* a dream! It's real!'

And then the Doctor gave a great shout of anger that startled them both.

'No!' he thundered. 'It is *not* real – don't believe that for an instant – don't be fooled into believing these tricks . . . There is no such thing as a unicorn – it's a legend, a mythical beast . . . You mustn't believe in a thing that doesn't exist . . . Repeat after me: it doesn't exist!'

Jamie and Zoe took a deep breath and uttered the words obediently: '*It doesn't exist!*'

The unicorn was almost on top of them – but at the sound of their voices it suddenly stopped in its tracks, and stood there, only a few feet away, completely motionless.

The Doctor walked up and touched it. 'As I thought . . . ' he said ruminatively. 'Some sort of stone – white marble perhaps? Not a living creature at all; merely the statue of a unicorn . . . Another test, sent to try us.'

Jamie blinked; his heart was still pounding, and his throat was dry. 'But - it *was* real,' he croaked. 'We all saw it.'

'It was terrifying,' Zoe agreed.

'We thought we saw it.' Patiently the Doctor tried to explain. 'He challenged us to believe in it. And if we had believed - it would have killed us.'

'You say "he" challenged us,' Zoe pursued. 'You mean the Master?'

'So I imagine . . . He seems to be the one responsible for setting up all these conjuring tricks.'

Jamie wiped his forehead: it was clammy and ice-cold - he had never felt so close to death. But all he could say was: 'I don't understand . . . I wish I did.'

The Doctor paced slowly round the statue of the unicorn, appraising it from all sides. 'This unicorn seemed to be real - until we declared that it wasn't. Once we all realised it was just another illusion, we were safe.'

'But we believed in it, Jamie and me,' Zoe reminded him.

'That was the danger: your belief was so strong, it almost convinced me as well. I had to hang on to logic, telling myself I must not believe the evidence of my own eyes. It was a very ingenious trap.'

Jamie shuddered: 'What kind of a mind would dream up a weird thing like that?'

The Doctor shrugged: 'I don't know - yet. But I suspect we shall soon find out. Whoever the Master is, he must be some kind of creative genius.'

(Safe at the centre of his spider's web of operations, in the heart of the Citadel, the Master watched a single monitor screen, and listened with gratification to the Doctor's tribute.

'Too kind, too kind,' he purred. 'And in all fairness I really must return the compliment! Our good friend the Doctor is obviously a man of supreme intelligence. He is learning the rules here with admirable speed . . . Go in a little closer - I want to get a better look at him.'

71

The image on the monitor screen slowly increased in size, as the Doctor's face shifted into a close-up.)

Zoe suppressed a cry of dismay, and tugged at the Doctor's sleeve. 'The soldiers!' she exclaimed. 'They're coming back.'

The Doctor looked round: straight into the ray of light which emanated from the lens on the toy soldier's helmet.

'Only one soldier this time,' he remarked. 'I wonder why.'

Then he spoke out boldly:

'Whoever you are – whatever you want – I accept your challenge.'

(In the Citadel, the Master rubbed his hands with glee. This was turning out even better than he had dared to hope. 'Splendid, splendid . . . I know now we were absolutely right to choose the Doctor . . . But there is no need to rush things. About turn – withdraw – and let the prisoners go free . . . For the time being.'

He was prolonging the suspense, quite deliberately: this battle of wits was so enjoyable, he wanted to keep it going as long as possible.

'After all,' he added, 'wherever they go, wherever they may try to hide, each step they take will only bring them nearer to us . . . The plot is hatched – the trap is set . . . All we have to do is wait – and let them walk into it . . . About turn! Quick march!')

Zoe and Jamie stayed close to the Doctor, and watched in amazement as the toy soldier stepped back, turned, and retreated in its usual left-right-left-right fashion – the key between its shoulderblades slowly unwinding as it moved off into the darkness.

'I wonder what happens when the clockwork runs down?' mused the Doctor. 'Does the Master wind them up again?'

'Why have they left us alone?' Zoe asked. 'What's going to happen?'

'Let's not wait to find out,' said Jamie quickly. 'Let's get out of here – as fast as possible . . . Come on!'

* * *

As Zoe pointed out, long afterwards: 'For three space travellers, used to covering vast distances through unknown galaxies, at speeds far greater than light – we seemed to spend an awful lot of time trudging along on our own flat feet in this adventure!'

Certainly, they did a great deal of walking: they left the black, empty plain behind them and struggled onwards without any clear idea of where they were going – or why. Some strange compulsion drove them on, and the Doctor tried to define what it was.

'Fear? No – it can't be that: because we don't know where we're going, and the greatest fear of all is the unknown . . . I'd say that the motive that keeps us going is curiosity. We want to find out what is going to happen next – it's as simple as that.'

As they walked, they talked: and Zoe remembered to tell her companions of the strange experience she had, just before she fell down that never-ending hole in the ground – when she found that her silver jump-suit had been replaced for a time by an old-fashioned blue dress, and a ribbon in her hair, and high-buttoned boots.

'You must have looked like Alice in Wonderland,' the Doctor realised.

They did not know what he was talking about – for Jamie had been born long before Lewis Carroll wrote about Alice's adventures, and Zoe, whose education had never included classics of literature, had not heard of the young lady either.

The Doctor tried to explain: 'Alice is a fictional character, just like the unicorn – and, I suspect, our eighteenth-century friend in the three-cornered hat . . . We're exploring a world of fiction and fable, where nothing is completely real.'

Jamie interrupted: 'You mean – these woods we're coming to – yon bushes and shrubbery – they're not there at all?'

For by now they had reached a grassy upland, where the stony floor of the plain gave way to lush vegetation. Exotic wildflowers blossomed on all sides, and they soon had to push their way through a thick underbrush, with rich green leaves and overhanging creepers.

Zoe sniffed: 'It's warm and wet . . . like a tropical rain forest.'

The Doctor agreed: 'The setting for an adventure story set in a fantastic jungle, no doubt.'

Brightly-coloured birds – macaws and parakeets – fluttered through the trees with startlingly shrill voices – and at one moment a huge plant with lurid fleshy petals, fringed with sticky hairs, snapped shut as they passed it, making them all jump.

'An author's overheated imagination must have dreamed that up,' said the Doctor with mild disdain. 'Venus Flytraps don't ever grow to that size – it was obviously meant to be a man-eating orchid!'

'I'm certainly glad it's not real,' said Jamie, with feeling. 'And I suppose – this face I've got that isna my face at all – that's not real either? Well, that's some comfort, I reckon.'

The further they went into the jungle, the more dense it became, and they had to force their way through thick screens of leaves, and – 'Ugh!' cried Zoe, with disgust. 'Spider's webs!'

The filmy grey webs stuck to her fingers, and she wiped them on a large green leaf – then shivered in dismay as a furry body with eight shaggy legs scuttled away crossly, its hiding place disturbed.

'I don't like this place,' she said plaintively. 'Can't we get into another story soon?'

'Don't despair,' said the Doctor, peering through the riot of tropical vegetation. 'There seems to be some sort of building just ahead of us . . . A ruined Inca temple, possibly?'

But when they finally pressed through into a little clearing in the forest, and the building was revealed, they found out that the Doctor's guess was wrong.

'It's a different story altogether,' he concluded. 'In a different time and place – an old-fashioned mystery novel, by the look of it.'

There was a splendid mansion, with a row of white pillars holding up the main portico, and long, louvred shutters to the windows on either side. But the house had seen better days: the stucco was crumbling and flaking away – the shutters needed a coat of fresh paint, and some of them were hanging askew, half off their hinges. The building was set among thick trees and shrubs – magnolia and rhododendron – that were a riot of vivid blossom, and seemed to be encroaching upon the house as if they would swallow it up.

'I wonder who lived here,' the Doctor pondered aloud. 'Some strange, tortured heroine of romance, I'd imagine . . . From the pen of a passionate female novelist!'

'There's only one way to find out,' said Jamie, and he bounded up the three cracked steps that led to the front door. Taking the brass knocker in his hand, he gave it a loud thump, and waited for a moment, then called out: 'Is there anybody there?'

Nobody came, and nobody answered. Only a bird flew up out of a turret above the traveller's head; and he smote upon the door a second time.

'Is there anybody there?' he said.

(The Doctor gave a little nod of recognition: he had read that poem by Walter de la Mare, once upon a time, long, long ago.)

But the second summons had been more successful than the first: for this time there was the squeak of a rusty bolt being drawn, and the click of a lock turning – and the front door swung open, protesting, upon its hinges.

Jamie recoiled in alarm – but it was too late.

For there, inside the door, stood the same Redcoat soldier he had encountered when he first arrived in this confusing place – with the same flintlock musket aimed at his head.

Jamie wasn't going to show he was afraid – that was certain.

'So it's you again!' he shouted. 'Well, this time, I'll take care of you for sure! *Creag an Tuire!*'

And with his war cry, he drew out his sheathknife to defend himself.

75

As before, the soldier fired the musket: there was a loud bang, and a cloud of white smoke . . . And when it cleared, the Redcoat had vanished, and in Jamie's place was a two-dimensional cut-out . . . A storybook illustration of a boy in a kilt – but a boy without a face.

Zoe gave a cry of grief and terror:

'Oh, no – *Jamie* – oh, Doctor, what have they done to him?'

The Doctor patted her shoulder comfortingly, and said, 'It's not as bad as you think . . . Don't worry – we'll soon put this right.' He looked up into the heavens impatiently, saying to whomsoever might be listening, 'Well, come on, come on – if you want to play games, let's get on with it!'

Was there a faint echo of laughter, far away, in reply – or was it just the wind sighing in the treetops?

Zoe pointed: 'Whatever is *that*?'

The Doctor turned: in the doorway stood the familiar blackboard and easel, with its identikit collection of scraps from a score of photographs.

'It's perfectly simple,' he explained to Zoe. 'All I have to do is put Jamie's face together again.'

'*Again*?' She looked at the photographic scraps – then, accusingly, at the Doctor. 'You mean you did this before?'

'Well – uh – yes . . . '

'And that's how Jamie's face got all changed – you made a mess of it, didn't you?'

The Doctor defended himself: 'No, no – I wouldn't say that – it was quite a creditable effort – for a first attempt. I happened to be a little rushed, that's all . . . Now, let me see – his eyes – which are his eyes?'

He started to choose a likely pair; but Zoe stopped him and handed him the correct ones. The Doctor cleared his throat: 'Ah, yes – I know, I know – don't keep interfering . . . '

Between them, they sorted out the various features that made up Jamie's face, and put them together on the blank cut-out.

Immediately the two dimensions increased to three: Jamie resumed his shape and stature, and came to life again – this time, with his own face. Zoe hugged him thankfully.

'Oh, Jamie – thank goodness you're back!'

'Back?' He stared at her. 'What d'ye mean – "back"? I haven't been anywhere . . . '

The Doctor smilingly produced his pocket-mirror again, as Zoe explained: 'You've got your face back.'

'I have?' Jamie checked his reflection and grinned broadly. 'Aye – so I have . . . That's a lot better.'

With renewed confidence, he indicated the front door which still stood half-open, and suggested: 'What d'ye say we explore inside the house? You never know – we might find out a bit more about what's going on.'

The Doctor agreed, and they all entered the ramshackle mansion. As they walked in, the front door swung slowly shut behind them.

They looked about them: the sight that met their eyes was very curious – a high-ceilinged hall, lit by antique candelabra, with flickering flames that guttered into trickles of wax.

'There must be somebody here,' Zoe pointed out. 'Someone had to light the candles.'

She looked around nervously – and gasped, as a sudden flurry of movement caught her eye. At one end of the hall was a long table, covered in a damask cloth that had once been white, but was now discoloured with dust and grime. At the head of the table stood a wedding cake: it had been there for years, and had long since gone mouldy – only its thick sugar icing held it together, in three grand tiers that had begun to topple at a precarious angle. Cobwebs veiled it, from the topmost wreath of orange blossom to the ceremonial knife, laid out ready to cut the cake – a knife that was never used.

And at the heart of the cake, a family of mice had made their nest: they twitched their tails and disappeared at the sight of the newcomers.

Zoe shuddered: 'A wedding cake that was never cut . . . '

'For a wedding that never took place,' the Doctor completed her sentence. 'But that's another story – by a chap called Dickens – you wouldn't know about him either, I'm afraid . . . Shall we proceed?'

Jamie had ventured a little further, and now reported back: 'There are four passages leading out of this hall – and four flights of stone steps that all seem to lead downwards . . . Into the cellars by the look of it . . . It'd be very easy to get lost in a place like this.'

'Just a moment!' The Doctor stooped, and picked up a small round object which lay at his feet. 'A ball of twine . . . This must be an invitation.'

'What do you mean?'

'It's the classic method of finding the way through a maze. Jamie – take the end of the string and tie it to the door.'

Jamie did as he was told – and then made an unpleasant discovery.

'Hey – this door isn't just shut . . . It's locked!'

Zoe looked at the Doctor apprehensively: 'You think we're meant to go on, don't you? Down into the cellars? You believe that wherever we go – whatever we do – they're expecting us?'

'It seems to be a reasonable supposition,' agreed the Doctor. 'Come along – let's make a start. And Jamie – you pay out the twine as we go – but whatever happens, don't let go of it!'

(In the Control Centre, the Master had momentarily abandoned the bank of monitors in favour of a new toy – a round screen, rather like a radar installation: a high-pitched eletronic blip sounded each time the radar arm swept across it.

What it showed was a cross-section of a complex maze – a tangle of passages, leading to one clear area at the very centre. And there were three moving dots of light, slowly making their way into the maze, inch by inch.

The Master clucked approvingly as he watched their progress.

'Ah, yes – the good Doctor is commendably prompt . . . I wonder how long it will take him to get to the heart of the mystery.')

It was certainly very difficult. The flight of stone steps had led the three explorers into an underground warren of tunnels which seemed to be carved out of solid rock. Each tunnel led in turn to another – dark alleys opened up left and right and at every few steps they had to stop and decide which way to go, as Jamie continued to unwind his ball of thread.

'Which way now, I wonder?' the Doctor asked, when they reached yet another junction.

'To the right,' said Zoe firmly.

'How can you be so sure?' he wanted to know. 'Both ways look equally unattractive to me.'

'It must be to the right – I've been working it out . . . It soon fell into a clear pattern. Once we avoided the dead ends, it was easy enough – first right, second left, third right, fourth left and so on . . . A simple arithmetic progression.'

The Doctor smiled admiringly: 'What it is to have a mathematical brain.'

Jamie interrupted: 'That's all very well – but I have news for you . . . The twine's run out.' He showed them that they had got to the end of the thread. 'D'ye think we should go back?'

The Doctor made up his mind quickly: 'No, Jamie – you stay here – Zoe and I will explore a little further. There must be a way out of this place, and I'd rather like to find it.'

Zoe said quietly: 'Perhaps they don't want us to find a way *out*? Only a way *in* . . .'

But they continued with their plan of campaign, leaving Jamie standing on guard. He didn't much fancy the idea of waiting, alone, in these underground passages, and he tried to whistle to keep his spirits up – but his lips were dry.

(On the radar screen, the Master noticed that one of the three dots of light had stopped, leaving the other two to go on towards the centre. He felt sure that the Doctor must be one of the exploring duo, and urged him on excitedly: 'Yes – yes – don't stop now - you're almost there!'

The dots of light flickered on – into the centre of the maze.)

* * *

79

It was a roughly circular chamber, hewn out of the rock, lit by one flickering torch stuck in an iron sconce on the wall, which threw leaping shadows. Zoe and the Doctor moved forward, and found themselves in the dead centre of the maze. She whispered: 'I was right . . . It isn't a way out – it's a dead-end . . . I don't like it – let's go back.'

'Yes, yes – in a moment,' the Doctor tried to reassure her. 'I was rather expecting another welcoming committee – possibly I was wrong . . . But there must have been someone here, not so long ago – look at the footprints on the floor.'

Zoe looked down: it was hard to see in the flickering torchlight, but . . . 'They don't look like footprints to me,' she said. 'More like the tracks of an animal – oh, Doctor!'

She broke off, her voice shaking; the flickering half-light picked out a pile of bones and a human skull . . . She clutched at his arm, saying, 'I know it's silly, but I keep remembering the story of the Minotaur . . . You know? It was half a man, half a bull – and it lived at the heart of a labyrinth – and there were human sacrifices . . . '

The Doctor patted her hand: 'Yes, my dear – but I don't think we need to be alarmed. After all, we do know that the Minotaur is only a – '

But Zoe wasn't listening. She was staring in horror at the opposite wall of rock. There was a light in the tunnel, and it threw up a gigantic shadow: the shadow of a misshapen creature with broad shoulders, and a vast, powerful head – and on that head was a pair of horns . . . The horns of a bull.

A few hundred yards away, in the dark, empty tunnel, Jamie still stood at his post.

He was cold and he was scared, and he was fed up with standing still: he wished very much that he could have stayed with the others – but what was the good of wishing? Somebody had to keep guard over the end of the thread, otherwise they'd never get out of this miserable place.

Oh, well – at least if he had to wait, he might as well make himself comfortable.

He sat down on a heap of stones: but that wasn't very

pleasant – the stones were cold and wet, and they had very sharp edges. What he needed was a cushion. He decided to improvise, and took off his jacket, rolling it up into a bundle: he would sit on that instead.

Feeling slightly more comfortable, he tried to whistle again – and this time succeeded in producing the ghost of an old Scottish tune: one that he remembered his brothers and sisters dancing to in the barn at home. He whistled the tune as cheerily as he could, casting his mind back to memories of happy family parties – the village *caelidh*, long ago and far away . . .

The melody faltered and went out of tune, as he felt a lump in his throat. It was a mistake to remember the old days too clearly. You had to look ahead: you must never look back.

The silence that followed seemed even more oppressive than before . . . But was it an unbroken silence? He thought he heard something, in the distance . . . A strange bellowing sound – but so far off, he couldn't be sure if he was imagining it. These winding tunnels played strange tricks on your ears, setting up all kinds of echoes and re-echoes.

He cupped his hands to his mouth and called: 'Doctor? Zoe! Are you all right?'

Then he waited; But there was no response: nothing but the dripping of water from the stone ceiling to the rocky floor below.

'Doctor! What's happening?' he called again.

This time there was an answer of sorts: and one that made the hairs on the back of his neck bristle. He heard the unmistakeable sound of marching feet: the noise of the toy soldiers – coming towards him.

He held his breath and tried to make himself invisible, pressing back against the cold, damp wall of rock.

The tramp of feet grew nearer, and then he saw a beam of light approaching.

One mechanical soldier came into view, stamping towards him along the tunnel. It turned its head from side to side, and the beams of light from its helmet lens raked the stone walls.

Jamie shrank still further back, and the beam of light crossed him – stopped – shifted back, as if it were looking for him. Jamie crouched down, and the light swung from side to side, before picking him out again.

Jamie looked up – and understood.

'Is that how you can find me? With that wee lighthouse of yours?'

(On the monitor screen, the Master watched, fascinated, as the young lad gazed straight into the light – they remained face to face for a moment, as if they were looking into each other's eyes.)

'So that's it,.' Jamie said. 'That's how you see . . . '

Then, in one swift movement, he picked up his jacket from the floor, and shook it out, holding it at arms-length, as a bullfighter holds out his cape – and suddenly flung it upwards and forwards, over the soldier's helmet, shrouding the magnesium ray.

(In the Control Centre, the Master gave a cry of rage as the screen went blank: 'You brainless idiot! Get yourself free, throw it off. Don't let the boy escape!')

But while the toy soldier threshed around blindly, Jamie took to his heels; he abandoned the ball of twine, and made a run for it. He didn't know where he was going – he only knew he had to get away.

The sound of his running footsteps echoed down the tunnel: but they were soon blotted out by another, much more terrifying sound.

Jamie listened; and his blood ran cold. There was no doubt about it this time.

Deep in the heart of the labyrinth, he heard the sound of a mighty roar: the roar of a crazed animal, about to devour its prey.

6

The Facts of Fiction

Within the hollow chamber at the centre of the labyrinth, the noise was almost over-powering.

The Doctor and Zoe shrank away instinctively, and he put a protective arm around her shoulders. He could feel her slender frame trembling, as the unearthly sound continued: the cry of an enraged monster.

It grew even louder, and the terrifying shadow at the mouth of the tunnel rose up like a thundercloud as the beast approached.

At last it emerged into the chamber: a grotesque and loathsome figure.

The Minotaur was, as Zoe had said, half-man, half-bull. From the shoulders down it appeared to be a man – a man with strong, muscular forearms and a barrel-like chest. Two massive legs like tree trunks supported this brawny torso, and it moved into the dancing torchlight with a deliberate, heavy tread.

But above the shoulders it was a bloodthirsty animal. A bull's square-browed head, with two red eyes, and wickedly-curving horns which sprang from a tangle of dense, matted hair . . . It eyed the two strangers balefully, and snorted, taking in a deep, rattling breath before opening its jaws and bellowing again.

The sound was deafening, and Zoe instinctively put her hands over her ears.

The Minotaur lowered its evil head, and – although its lower limbs seemed human enough – it made a disturbingly animal movement, pawing the sandy floor of the cave with one naked foot.

'It's coming closer – ' Zoe exclaimed, and her voice sounded thin and faint against the sheer volume of blaring sound. 'It's going to attack us!'

The Doctor tried to sound confident as he reminded her: 'It's only another trick, Zoe . . . Remember - the Minotaur is a legend, another mythical beast, like the unicorn.'

She interrupted him desperately: 'It's *there* - I see it. *I'm frightened*!'

And the Doctor realised that with her hands over her ears, she could not hear what he said. All she could do was stare in horror as the nightmarish beast lumbered towards them - and she was convinced that she was about to be killed.

The Doctor grabbed her wrists and forced her hands down, shouting urgently: 'Listen to me, Zoe! The Minotaur is a mythical beast - it does not exist - '

'No . . . ' She shook her head, whimpering with fear. 'I don't believe you . . . '

He pulled her roughly towards him, shielding her with his own body as the monster moved in for the kill.

'You will obey me!' the Doctor commanded her harshly. 'Repeat after me: the Minotaur is a mythical beast - it does not exist!'

Zoe gazed into the Doctor's eyes, and under his almost mesmeric influence, she found herself repeating in a whisper: '*The Minotaur is a mythical beast - it does not exist* . . . '

The silence came so abruptly, that it was like a physical blow. The roaring ceased instantly, and the black shadow that had been looming over them disappeared. Fearfully, Zoe turned her head - and found that the chamber was empty. The light from the torch on the wall continued to flicker and leap, but it illuminated no horrid spectacle.

The nightmare was over.

'It's really gone - for good?' She felt weak with relief.

The Doctor gave a small, tentative smile: 'I'm afraid that when the poor brute realised that we would not accept his existence we made it impossible for him to stay . . . Now, I suggest we should make our way back along the tunnel to find Jamie.'

'Yes - oh, yes . . . I can't wait to get out of this hateful place,' Zoe agreed, and they set off together, back along the tunnel.

It wasn't that far, after all. The Doctor recognised certain shapes in the rock formation – and when they reached a point where the tunnel split off in three different directions, he stopped.

'I'm almost sure this is the spot where – ' Then he hesitated.

'Yes, I'm certain you're right,' said Zoe. 'I remember that big stone – it looks a bit like a giant snailshell – I noticed it before.'

'Possibly a form of fossil – an oversized ammonite,' the Doctor agreed. 'But I'm afraid Jamie's not here.'

Zoe frowned: 'Surely he wouldn't go off on his own without . . . ' She saw the expression on the Doctor's face. 'What's the matter?'

By way of reply, he stopped, and picked up the rough tweed jacket which he had noticed, thrown aside in a dark corner.

'He was here . . . But he seems to have left in rather a hurry.'

They looked at each other uneasily, and the Doctor added, with as much confidence as he could muster: 'We'd better look for him – I'm sure he can't be far away.'

'Jamie?' Zoe called. 'Can you hear me?'

Her voice echoed eerily along the miles of subterranean passages: and a moment later, as if in reply, they heard footsteps approaching.

'Thank goodness – here he comes now!' she exclaimed joyfully. 'Jamie – we thought we'd lost you . . . '

But her words tailed off as the newcomer appeared around the side of the giant, fossilised shell. It was the eighteenth-century traveller in the three-cornered hat.

'Oh . . . ' she said, unable to hide her disappointment. 'It's you.'

However, the traveller hailed them cheerfully, and the Doctor seemed pleased to see him, saying: 'My dear fellow – you have a knack of turning up at the most unexpected moments!'

Zoe didn't bother with social courtesies – she swept these

greetings aside and got down to brass tacks: 'Have you seen Jamie?'

The stranger shook his head, saying: 'I walked alone, and saw no sign of any inhabitants.'

'Are you absolutely positive?'

He seemed a little affronted: 'I would not impose any falsities upon you – I adhere strictly to truth.'

The Doctor interposed hastily: 'I'm sure Zoe didn't mean to imply any – um – er – let's change the subject, shall we? Tell me, this person you described to us – the one who controls everything hereabouts – I believe you referred to him as – '

'The Master – yes?'

'Have you ever met him personally?'

The stranger smiled, a shade uneasily: 'Upon occasion, he has been pleased to grant me an audience.'

'Ah . . . And where might I find him?'

'The Master's palace is no regular edifice, but a citadel like a walled town, at the top of a hill or cliff which is reckoned the highest in the Kingdom.'

The Doctor seemed to be delighted with this answer; Zoe could not understand why he chuckled to himself, as if enjoying a private joke. 'Quite so, quite so – my dear sir, I think I begin to understand you,' he smiled. 'And might I ask where you come from? Would it perhaps be – from Nottingham?'

The man pushed back his three-cornered hat in amazement, and conceded that this shot in the dark had struck the bullseye indeed.

'My father had a small estate in Nottinghamshire: I was the third of five sons. He sent me to Emmanuel College in Cambridge at fourteen years old, where I applied myself close to my studies – learning navigation and other parts of the mathematics, useful – '

The Doctor chimed in eagerly: 'Useful to those who intend to travel?'

And the two men concluded in chorus, repeating the words together: ' . . . As I always believed it would be, some time or other, my fortune to do!'

The Doctor slapped his new-found friend on the back, exclaiming heartily: 'Now I know you, sir! Your name, I believe is, Gulliver . . . Mr Lemuel Gulliver?'

'Your servant, sir!' cried Mr Gulliver joyfully, and they shook hands on it.

'*Gulliver*? But that's not – ' Zoe tried to cut in, but the Doctor silenced her with a warning look and a finger to his lips.

'Ssh! My dear chap – I look forward to having a long talk with you, one of these days.'

Gulliver was delighted. 'I should like it above all things . . . But it would not be proper, at this juncture, to trouble you with the particulars of my adventures.'

'No, you're quite right – we mustn't detain you.'

'Having been condemned by Nature and Fortune to an active and restless life, I must take my leave of you. Farewell!'

He bowed once more to them both, then turned and walked off along the passage, the way he had come.

Zoe felt her head whirling after such a torrent of words: 'I'm sure he means well – but why does he talk in such an extraordinary way?'

The Doctor still had a half-smile on his lips as he gazed along the tunnel and replied: 'Because, my dear girl, he can only speak the words that Dean Swift gave him to· say. Whatever sentences he utters, I'm quite sure you'll find them somewhere in the pages of *Gulliver's Travels*. Without that book, he would be speechless.'

'That's ridiculous!' Zoe was beginning to feel quite indignant. 'How can he be Gulliver? There never was any such person as Gulliver – he's a made-up character in a novel – '

'Of course he is. I keep trying to explain to you – this world we've tumbled into is a world of fiction . . . Unicorns – Minotaurs – Lemuel Gulliver – they're all alive and well and living upon this strange planet.'

'But what are they doing here? And what are *we* doing here? What do they want with us?'

'That's something I don't know – yet . . . But I'm determined to find out. Just as I'm determined to solve another little problem.'

'What problem?'

'The whereabouts of Jamie . . . Come along – let's be on our way. The sooner we find him, the better!'

And throwing Jamie's tweed jacket over his shoulder, the Doctor led the way along yet another underground passage.

The Doctor and Zoe were not to know, of course, that Jamie was no longer underground.

When he first tried to escape from the toy soldier, he had run as fast as his legs could carry him along the tunnels, not caring which way he went, concentrating only on getting away.

The rocky passages got smaller and steeper, and soon he found himself in almost total darkness, brought up short time and again by sharp projections of stone or low, overhanging boulders. He bruised his arms and legs painfully, and more than once hit his head on a sudden slope in the roof above him.

The pursuing toy soldier had none of these disadvantages – Jamie could hear its relentless marching feet coming closer and closer, and a metallic clang every time it struck against the stone walls. And of course the soldier had another great advantage over Jamie: the round reflector on its helmet threw out a permanent beam of light so that it could always see the way ahead clearly illuminated, as if in the head-lamps of a car.

In consequence, the soldier never slackened pace for an instant – while Jamie – sore, stumbling and out of breath – found himself getting slower and slower.

But just as it seemed capture was inevitable, he had a stroke of luck. He collided with the rock yet again, cursing under his breath, and sucking his grazed knuckles – then dodged back against the wall, as the rock, which he had dislodged, came hurtling down, bringing a minor avalanche of stones, pebbles and gravel after it.

For a terrible moment, he thought that the whole tunnel was going to cave in, for the fall of stones went on and on: he was protected by an overhanging ledge, but feared he might be walled up alive.

Then at last the downfall stopped: and – wonder of wonders! – he saw a ray of sunlight, with dust-motes dancing in it. He pressed forward, scrambling over the mound of rubble which he had accidentally created, ducked under a jagged edge of stone, and found himself out in the fresh air again.

The underground passages had led him out among a wilderness of boulders, at the foot of an enormous cliff.

Somewhere behind him, inside the rocky passage, he could hear the noise of the toy soldier still doggedly coming after him: though a little slowed down by having to pick its way over the fallen debris.

Jamie realised with a sudden surge of hope that although the toy soldiers could march rapidly over level terrain, they wouldn't be much good at climbing!

He glanced up at the towering cliff above him, and remembered the summer days of his boyhood, when he and his brothers used to go rock-climbing in the Scottish Highlands. If he could do it then, he could do it now. He set off as nimbly as a young mountain goat, and began to scale the cliff.

Below him, the toy soldier emerged from the cave mouth that had newly opened up and began to follow him . . . But as Jamie had guessed, the soldier's flat feet were not made for scrambling over boulders, and after two or three attempts the wretched clockwork toy slipped backwards and landed on its back with a reverberating, tinny crash.

The giant key in its back stopped revolving: the spring had finally run down.

A moment later, the light-beam that shone from its helmet reflector was switched off. (The Master pressed a button, seated at his Control Panel, and muttered irritably: 'Out of service . . . Send for replacements.') For the time being, it seemed that Jamie was free from danger.

He was halfway up the cliff face by now, and after one brief glance back, over his shoulder, he had remembered that you must never, never look down when you're rock-climbing. Besides – he couldn't go back. The only way open to him now was onward and upward . . . But how?

The problem was: he'd have to be a human fly to ascend the upper half of the cliff face. It was a sheer vertical slab, with no visible projection or handhold to help him.

Jamie stayed where he was – on an uncomfortably narrow ledge – and tried to think what he should do next.

'I can't climb that – and I daren't go back down . . . Of course what I really need now is a – '

He was about to say 'a rope', but as he spoke he found that his wish had been granted even before the words left his mouth.

Looking up, he saw a thick, hairy rope snaking down the cliff face towards him. He grinned happily: 'Who says wishes don't come true?'

And he grabbed the rope with both hands, and hung on tightly. It seemed firm enough, so he decided to risk it. Somebody, somewhere, wanted him to get to the top of the cliff – very well, he wouldn't disappoint them.

Bracing his feet against the wall of rock, he began to make his way up the rope, hand over hand.

It was a long climb, and his arm muscles were soon aching, but he knew he couldn't give up. Slowly he made the ascent, like an insect crawling up a window pane. The sweat stood out on his forehead, but he gritted his teeth and struggled on, very conscious of the sheer drop that lay below.

He would not look back – and he preferred not to look up either, but stared fixedly at the unfriendly surface of smooth rock as it slid by, inch by inch. Consequently, he was not prepared for the surprise that awaited him at the top.

The rock turned to slabs of stone, carefully built into a solid wall – and the wall in turn was set back to include an old-fashioned mullioned window, deep in the thickness of the stonework.

Now at last Jamie glanced up – and realised that the rocky heights of the cliff were surmounted by a vast medieval castle, with towers and turrets and battlements . . . Just like a castle in a storybook.

And the mullioned window stood half-open.

The rope Jamie had climbed disappeared through the window, and as his head and shoulders reached the stone windowledge, he gave the rope a final tug to make sure that it was still securely fastened.

To his amazement, a girl's voice responded with a cry of: *'Ouch!'*

And a second later, a beautiful girl appeared at the open window. She had long blonde hair, under a silver coronet, and a filmy, fairy tale dress – and Jamie realised with some embarrassment that her long blonde tresses were plaited into a long braid, and the long braid went on and on and eventually turned into the 'rope' which he had been climbing.

Now the beautiful girl regarded him with some severity, and said: 'I suppose you know that hurts.'

Jamie swallowed hard and said in a small voice: 'Oh, gosh – I mean – I'd no idea – I mean – is that really all *yours*?'

The fairy tale princess sighed: 'Of course it is. I don't mind people climbing – I'm quite used to it, actually . . . Only you would keep tugging so.'

'I'm awfully sorry,' Jamie apologised.

She dismissed this with a wave of her aristocratic hand, and then asked: 'Are you a prince?'

'No . . . Why?'

'You're supposed to be. I'm a princess – but you probably know that. My name is Rapunzel. I dare say you've heard of me: I'm quite well-known, as princesses go.'

Jamie frowned, holding on to the edge of the windowsill with his fingertips. This seemed a very extraordinary place to be having such an extraordinary conversation.

'Rapunzel . . . ' he mumbled. 'Aye, I reckon I've heard the name, but – '

'You're not a woodcutter's son, by any chance?'

'No, I'm the son of a piper, and my arms are getting tired, so – '

'A piper's son? You must be Tom!' she decided. 'I've heard of you too.'

'Wrong again, your Highness; my name's Jamie McCrimmon. My arms are just about to come out of their sockets, so if you don't mind – '

'Jamie McCrimmon?' She shook her head regretfully. 'No, I'm afraid I've never heard of you, Mr McCrimmon – how very disappointing. In that case I think you'd better go. Goodbye.'

She turned as if to move away and Jamie called desperately: 'But wait a minute, your Highness – Rapunzel. You can't leave me like this! If I let go I'll fall to the bottom of the cliff, and that would make a terrible mess . . . Please let me climb in through the window.'

She looked doubtful. 'I don't think it would be allowed.'

'I wouldn't stay long,' he panted, feeling his sweaty fingers beginning to slip on the smooth, hard stone. 'Just a brief visit – passing through, you understand. Please!'

Rapunzel eyed him appraisingly, then relented. 'Oh, very well . . . I must say it's a great pity you're not a prince – you'd have made rather a good one . . . Come along then – but for goodness sake keep quiet!'

She moved back from the window, and Jamie made one last determined effort, and succeeded in hauling himself up over the stone ledge.

He landed headfirst, in a heap on the floor, and then picked himself up, tugging his kilt into place and dusting himself down – not wishing to look too much of a fool in the eyes of the princess.

The princess? What princess?

Jamie looked around in bewilderment – for the Princess Rapunzel was nowhere to be seen. He blurted out: 'Princess – your Highness – where have you gone? This is no time to play hide and seek . . . '

His thoughts raced: not only had she disappeared but those yards and yards of blonde, plaited hair had vanished too – all within a split second. It was like a conjuring trick.

'A trick . . . Of course – another of those rotten tricks,' he realised bitterly: and came to the same conclusion that the Doctor and Zoe had reached about Lemuel Gulliver. 'But then she's a character in a fairytale – she's not a real live person at all.'

He sighed: she may only have been an illusion, but she was a very pretty illusion, and he would have liked to get to know her better . . . Oh, well – there was no point in crying over spilled milk now: he had reached the castle at any rate; he would have to explore it further. Then he frowned, and took a closer look at his surroundings.

This was like no castle he had ever seen. The inside of this strange building was very different from the outside. The room in which he found himself had no ancient stone walls, massive oak doors, or wrought-iron gates.

It was all smooth, shining and brightly lit from some concealed source in the polished ceiling. Walls and shelves and work surfaces everywhere were of some unknown plastic substance – and the whole place looked more like a laboratory than a fairy tale citadel. In fact, it resembled the heart of a gigantic computer or word processor – though Jamie could not have been expected to recognise such a thing.

He watched the tape decks spinning and whirring at irregular intervals: small lights flashed red and green – and it occurred to him that it was a little like the control panel of the ill-fated TARDIS.

In this random thought he was nearer the mark than he suspected – for, although he was unaware of the fact, this room was only a few yards away from the Control Centre – where, at that very moment the Master sat before his bank of television screens, and plotted his next move.

Another tape deck, which had been motionless, suddenly sprang into life at Jamie's elbow with a loud whirring sound, making him jump.

He took a pace back, putting out a hand to steady himself – and accidentally brushed against a switch which activated a microfilm projector. At once the screen on the opposite wall blazed with light, throwing up the image of a printed page – the first page of a book.

'Marley was dead, to begin with. There is no doubt whatever about that. The register of his burial was signed by the clergyman, the clerk, the undertaker, and the chief mourner. Scrooge signed it. And Scrooge's name was good upon 'change for anything he chose to put his hand to . . . Old Marley was as dead as a doornail.'

Jamie read these words with blank incomprehension: he had never heard of these people – just as he had never heard of Charles Dickens, or of *A Christmas Carol*. Who was Scrooge? Who was old Marley, and how had he died? Was this meant as some kind of warning?

He tried to turn the microfilm projector off again, but pressed the wrong switch. A cassette recorder began to operate, and as the twin spools revolved, a female voice from a nearby speaker made the hairs prickle at the back of Jamie's scalp . . . He whirled around in alarm – but there was nobody there. Just a recorded voice, which continued placidly:

' "Christmas won't be Christmas without any presents," grumbled Jo, lying on the rug . . . "It's so dreadful to be poor!" sighed Meg looking down at her old dress . . . "I don't think it's fair for some girls to have lots of pretty things and – " '

Click! Jamie found the right switch this time, and the voice was silenced in mid-sentence.

He looked again at the cassette in the machine and saw that it was labelled *Little Women*. Then he wandered on, searching the room for clues: every available corner was filled with shelves, all stacked with more cassettes and box-files – all neatly labelled in a scholarly hand: *Treasure Island; The Pit and the Pendulum; Swallows and Amazons; Alice in Wonderland*.

Slowly he began to realise that he was in some strange library, where all the stories ever written had been safely stored away, in endless memory banks.

Only they were not all stories that *had* been written: some of them were stories that had yet to be worked out. There were stories here that were still being composed, at this very moment.

(In the adjoining room, the Master picked up his pen and began to write . . .)

Jamie was startled yet again by another unfamiliar sound. He traced it to its source – a tickertape machine, tucked away in a side alcove, which clattered busily as it spewed forth a thin paper ribbon with words printed upon it.

Inquisitively, he read the sentence as it unrolled before his eyes: and felt a sudden chill of fear.

'The Doctor and Zoe, unable to find their companion in the labyrinth, came at last to an underground lake – where a new terror awaited them . . . '

'It seems to be an underground lake,' said the Doctor.

He and Zoe stood on the shore of the lake: at intervals around the lakeslde, rough niches had been carved out of the rock, and in each one stood a branched candelabrum. The candleflames illuminated the walls of the cave – huge columns of iridescent colour, formed by vast stalagmites and stalactites, like organ pipes, glowing with unearthly hues of red and ochre and gold. And the deep black waters at their feet reflected the scene in a perfect, unbroken mirror: two images, one reversed beneath the other – for the water was not ruffled by the least wave or ripple, but remained totally still, as if it were waiting . . .

'It looks sinister,' said Zoe at last. 'Let's go back – Jamie can't have got past this place – there's no way forward.'

'Oh yes, there is,' said the Doctor. 'Nothing has been left to chance.' And he indicated a flat-bottomed skiff, lying motionless alongside, tied up to a metal ring set into the rock.

'I think,' he continued, 'that we are meant to go on . . . not back.'

Zoe had a sudden moment of panic. 'No!' she said. 'It's all too easy – it's luring us on to something horrible – it's a trap!'

'This place is a collection of traps, one after another,'

replied the Doctor. 'So far we have come through them unscathed. And I can't bear to resign from the game now. I look forward to meeting this inventive games-player – whoever he is – face to face . . . Come along – don't be afraid.'

'I *am* afraid,' said Zoe in a small voice.

'I know . . . But come along anyway – that's what bravery means. If we were never afraid, there would be nothing to be brave about.'

As he spoke, the Doctor untied the painter and helped Zoe into the boat. Stepping in after her, he pushed off from the rocky shore, and their frail craft glided out into the middle of the deep, inky waters.

There were no oars, no rudder – nothing to propel the skiff – and yet it floated serenely on, as if it knew the way to go.

'You see? We were expected,' said the Doctor.

The lake was larger than they had at first thought, for when they circled around a rocky outcrop at the furthest point, they found that it opened up into another tunnel – a subterranean river, still glowing with an eerie light from the strategically placed candelabra.

The rock formations were breathtakingly beautiful: the colours were beyond belief. On they went – with the splendour of the geological display all around them gradually lulling their apprehensions.

'It's like a dream,' Zoe said at last. 'I feel as if we might sail on like this for ever. As if the dream will never end.'

But after a while, the boat seemed to change course. It floated towards the bank – and there it stopped, at the foot of a flight of stone steps: and would go no further.

'We have reached our destination, I fancy,' said the Doctor. 'Come on – let's go ashore, and see what new marvels are in store for us.'

They left the skiff behind them and climbed the steps. At the top, they found themselves in a small circular cavern, fenced in by yet more stalagmites, and lit by yet more branched candlesticks.

The cavern was empty, except for a marble statue at the

far end – the statue of a woman in Grecian draperies with thick sausage curls piled upon her marble head, looking rather like the Venus de Milo before she lost her arms.

The Doctor glanced at this piece of artwork with interest. 'What have we here?' he enquired. 'I imagine there must be at least one more test in store for us – do you suppose this statue is something to do with it?'

'I believe you're actually *enjoying* all this . . . ' Zoe accused him.

'Well, it *is* a challenge, isn't it?' the Doctor retorted. 'And the last statue we encountered was the unicorn so – '

He broke off, and frowned. 'Is it a trick of the light, or did you see the statue move?'

Zoe clutched his hand. 'It can't. Statues don't move.'

'Except the unicorn . . . That was alive and mobile, until it froze into a statue. But this time, I suspect the situation is reversed . . . '

Zoe swallowed hard. 'It's true – it's happening the other way around – the statue is coming to life!'

There was a definite movement in the marble figure now: no question about that. Slowly the female figure stretched her limbs, and advanced towards them. But the most terrifying part was the transformation of her hair – for on top of her noble brow, those thick sausage curls now seemed to have a life of their own. Each one began to writhe, wriggling and squirming; they raised their pointed heads and hissed, like a nest of serpents . . .

'The Medusa,' said the Doctor simply.

The dream had not ended yet: it had turned into a nightmare.

In his control centre, somewhere high above them, the Master chuckled with glee, and continued to write – his pen flashing across the paper.

In the adjoining room, quite unaware of this, Jamie continued to read the printed words that poured out on the ticker tape – his eyes wide with horror.

'Now the Doctor and the girl were face to face with the Medusa . . .

97

One glance from her eyes would turn them to stone.'

The Medusa continued to grope her way towards them – but blindly, for her marble eyes were still shut. At any moment, the heavy eyelids would raise and the fatal gaze of those bewitching eyes would fall upon them, petrifying them for all time . . .

The Doctor grabbed Zoe and pulled her roughly towards him, averting his own gaze from the monstrous creature that approached them.

'We know what we have to do,' he said, trying to keep his voice calm.

'Yes . . . ' Zoe whispered back. 'She's coming nearer – I can hear her footsteps . . . She's going to make us look at her.'

'There's nothing to be frightened of – you know that now. We have to say that the Medusa does not exist.'

'But she *does* – listen!'

It was a horrible sound: the laboured, heavy shuffle of stone limbs, dragging across a stone floor.

'Zoe, the Medusa is an ancient legend . . . You must not believe in her – you must not shake my disbelief – or she can turn us both to stone . . . Say after me – the Medusa does not exist – '

Zoe cried out as if she were in torment: 'She does, she does! She's alive, she's real!'

The marble creature was very close now: from the corner of his eye, the Doctor saw her stretch out a marble arm, the fingers of her hand spread out, reaching forward . . .

Touching Zoe's cheek with ice-cold fingertips, tracing the line of her jaw, cupping her chin . . .

Zoe gave a stifled scream, as the gorgon began to turn her face towards her and the Doctor shouted: 'Don't look into her eyes – *don't look*!'

7

'I Am The Karkus'

Somehow, Jamie knew this wasn't just another story. He could feel with total inner conviction, that the words he read on the endless ribbon of tickertape were describing a life-and-death struggle taking place at this very moment. And there was nothing he could do to help.

Nothing – except to go on reading the tape.

'*One glance from her eyes would turn them to stone . . . But all was not yet lost.*'

(What was this? A ray of hope at last? He read on, impatiently.)

'*Suddenly the Doctor found a sword at his feet. He picked it up, and with one stroke he slew the monster . . .*'

Zoe's face was held as if in a vice, by the stone fingertips. She kept her eyes tightly shut, clutching the Doctor's hand and uttering a desperate cry: 'I can feel her hands on me – freezing cold, like ice – '

'As cold as marble, Zoe – a marble statue. Don't look at her!' the Doctor repeated. 'Remember she's a legend, a fantasy.'

'I can't think any more. I must open my eyes, I've got to look at her – *I've got to!*'

The Doctor took a step back, trying to pull Zoe away from the monstrous thing that held her in its power. As he moved, his foot struck against something, something metallic, that scraped across the rocky floor and threw up sparks.

He looked down, and saw that it was a sword, as sharp as a razor, lying at his feet.

'A sword!' He tried to remember how Perseus had slain the Gorgon in Greek mythology . . . Didn't he cut her head off? 'Should I use the sword?' he wondered.

He picked it up in one swift movement: the blade was like

99

a rapier – lithe and springy. It would be over in a moment, he thought: he had only to use his courage and strike deep . . .

'Yes, yes: use the sword! That's what it's there for!' Zoe begged him. 'Please, Doctor – do it quickly . . . Do it now!'

Suddenly the Doctor gave a great cry, and hurled the sword away with all his strength. It struck the walls of the cavern with a mighty clang, setting off a score of ringing echoes.

'*No!*' The Doctor thundered. 'It's another trap – the most cunning of all these traps . . . How can I say that the Medusa does not exist, if I kill her? How can you kill something that doesn't exist? There must be another way! What did Perseus do – exactly?'

Then the answer came to him: 'Wait – I have it now – he looked at her reflection . . . We need a mirror, of course!'

With frantic haste, he pulled out a small mirror from his side pocket, and turned it until it was in front of the Medusa's face – the baleful glare of her eyes reflecting back directly at herself. Instantly, the merciless expression froze into immobility, and the Doctor exclaimed triumphantly: 'Open your eyes; Zoe, you're safe now!'

Zoe obeyed, and found herself staring with appalled fascination at the face of the Gorgon: the white marble features were harmless, the coiffure of writhing serpents stabbed and hissed no more: it was nothing but a lifeless piece of sculpture once again.

'She looked at her own reflection in the glass,' the Doctor explained, 'and so turned herself to stone.'

Zoe's head was swimming. She clung to the Doctor, hiding her face against his jacket.

'It's all right, my dear,' he told her gently. 'You've got nothing to be afraid of. The statue is only a statue.'

'Infernal damnation take the man!'

The Master threw down his pen in a fit of rage; then he tore the page of manuscript into tiny scraps.

'The good Doctor is too clever by half! I must find another

way to inveigle him. And this time, the trap must be fool-proof – with no possibility of escape.'

At the same moment, the ticker-tape machine in the next room clattered out one final message and then fell silent:

'Cancel cancel cancel . . . The Doctor test reports . . . failure.'

Jamie waited – but there was nothing more forthcoming. It seemed that – this time at least – the Doctor had got the upper hand.

Still puzzled, but more than a little relieved, Jamie scratched his head.

So far, so good! Now to get out of this bewildering place . . . There was a door set below an archway at the far end of the room, and he set off towards it at a brisk pace.

What he did not notice – and even if he had, he would certainly not have understood its purpose – was a narrow beam of light, a few inches above the floor level, which shone on to a photo-electric cell.

As he crossed the beam, breaking the circuit, an alarm bell was set off – piercingly loud, jangling a warning for all to hear.

Jamie stopped short, and retreated in dismay: which meant that he recrossed the beam of light and broke the circuit again. A second bell, with a deeper, more threatening tone, added its clangour to the first.

Looking about wildly for a way of escape, Jamie saw the open window through which he had climbed. There seemed to be no alternative – he would have to take his chances on that perilous cliff face again.

He made for the window – but as he reached it, a steel grille slid down like a shutter: he was caught.

To add to his discomfiture, a disembodied, metallic voice now made an announcement from all the loudspeakers in the room: *'Attention, attention! There is a stranger in the building . . . Guard to search all areas immediately!'*

Jamie thought fast: he couldn't get out of the window, but he didn't mean to stay here like a cornered rat – the door was his only hope. At least he couldn't make matters worse by setting off any more alarm bells.

He ran towards the archway – and at the same instant, the door opened and the traveller in the three-cornered hat strolled in, smiling as if he had not a care in the world.

'Look out – ' Jamie began instinctively, seeing that he was about to cross the electric beam.

But Gulliver walked through the ray of light without breaking it: and then Jamie realised with a sickening pang that this eighteenth-century gentleman threw no shadow . . . So he, too, was just another illusion.

But now Lemuel Gulliver strode up and shook him warmly by the hand, saying: 'Ah! The young traveller – I had wondered as much.'

Jamie asked suspiciously: 'Have you been sent to find me?'

Gulliver nodded: 'His companions were in a state of some anxiety concerning his present whereabouts.'

'Companions? You mean Zoe and the Doctor. Where are they?'

'Safe and in good health.'

'That's a relief . . . You've actually spoken to them?'

'The gentleman desired I would let him know what place I came from, and whither I was bound.'

Jamie began to relax: illusion or no, this chap seemed to be friendly enough. But before he could question him further about the Doctor he became distracted by a sound, somewhere outside the room . . . An unearthly whirring noise: he seemed to recognise it – he felt sure he had heard it before, but he couldn't remember where . . .

'What's that?' he asked – straining his ears.

Gulliver listened, then shook his head: 'I heard nothing.'

'There – can't you hear it now? It's getting louder . . . ' Suddenly Jamie knew why it seemed so horribly familiar: it was the eerie, electronic hum created by the White Robots – the first creatures he had encountered in this hallucinatory place. He shuddered, and exclaimed: 'So that's the search party they're sending out to look for me . . . '

'By the laws of this kingdom, every chamber must be searched,' Gulliver agreed, apologetically.

'Aye – and if they find me, I'm done for.'

'You should be put to death . . . ' Gulliver frowned, unwilling to countenance such a fate for his young friend. He looked about, and found a solution.

There was a central table in the room, covered with technological equipment – and below the table was a long low storage cupboard, with sliding doors. Without wasting any words, Gulliver slid these doors open, and indicated to Jamie that he should take cover inside.

'But what about you?' Jamie asked.

'I should come to no harm,' Gulliver reassured him, and urged him into the hiding-place.

'Well – all right then – but if you give me away this time, I'm finished!' muttered Jamie, scrambling into the cupboard.

'I was ready, with the hazard of my life, to defend his person,' said Gulliver firmly.

Then he slid the door shut, and perched himself upon the edge of the table, with his legs swinging in front of the cupboard – and he whistled a little tune as he waited.

The sounds of the electronic vibrations were very strong now: and a moment later the door opened, and three White Robots advanced into the room. They stood there, side by side, slowly turning their heads as they surveyed the scene. They scrutinised Gulliver, then ignored him.

Gulliver's reaction was eerie indeed – for he could not see these intruders, but gazed through them as if they did not exist, which, for him, they did not.

The White Robots moved as one, and advanced down the length of the room. As they reached the far end, a warning red light began to flash, and a series of shrill 'bleeps' emerged from the loudspeakers. Then a section of the wall slid back, revealing a velvety darkness beyond. The White Robots moved on, into the darkness, and the wall slid back into place once more.

Gulliver had been kicking his heels, staring into space through all this, and seeing nothing. Silence fell.

After a cautious moment, the cupboard door opened

steathily, and Jamie poked his head out. 'Where have they gone? The White Robots?' he asked.

Gulliver laughed: 'Young sir, I do assure you – there were no such persons here.'

Jamie scrambled to his feet, and stood shaking out his kilt: there was no point in starting an argument about it, that was quite clear. 'Yes – well – Robots or no Robots – how am I going to get out of this place?'

He walked moodily across to the grille, now firmly in place at the open window, and rattled the bars.

'You desire your liberty?' enquired Gulliver.

'You could say that,' Jamie agreed bitterly. 'I got in here easily enough – the question now is: how do I get out?'

Gulliver appeared to be giving this question his earnest attention: he furrowed his brow, and remained deep in thought for several moments. At last he began: 'After some consideration . . . ' And then he paused.

'Yes – what?' Jamie prompted him. 'After some consideration . . . ?'

'I was of the opinion that . . . ' Another, even longer, pause.

'Well, go on – say it!' said Jamie, in a frenzy of impatience.

Gulliver took a deep breath, and finished: 'After some consideration – I was of the opinion – that this was altogether impossible.'

Jamie exploded with disappointment and frustration.

'Thanks for nothing! You're a great help! . . . I just wish the Doctor was here – he knows all the answers!'

Far below at the foot of the cliff, where scattered rocks lay around the newly uncovered exit from the underground labyrinth, the Doctor and Zoe rubbed their eyes, blinking in the unexpected glare of daylight.

They had been travelling through the bowels of the earth, like moles, for so long – they could not at first accustom themselves to so much light: and now they had finally made their way out through the new opening (unwittingly created by Jamie, had they but known it) they both had some trouble in focussing upon the prospect before them.

'It's a mountainside!' exclaimed Zoe, looking up in dismay, and tilting her head further and further back. 'Look at it – it goes straight up for miles and miles . . .'

'I've told you a thousand times – you must not exaggerate,' the Doctor reproved her mildly. But he followed her gaze, and screwed up his eyes again. 'Good gracious me – look up there, right at the top of the cliff . . . Is this just another illusion, or do you see what I see?'

Zoe's vision was blurred; a kaleidoscope of towers and turrets, domes and battlements swam crazily together and settled slowly into place.

'It – it looks like an old medieval castle,' she said doubtfully.

'Of course! The citadel!' The Doctor clapped his hands. 'Now we're getting warmer at last . . . Don't you remember, our friend Gulliver referred to the Master as living in "no regular edifice, but a citadel like a walled town, at the top of a hill or cliff which is reckoned the highest in the kingdom" . . . This must be the place!'

'You think the Master's up there?' Zoe asked.

'I'm quite certain of it. It won't be long before we meet him face to face – I must say I can hardly wait.'

'Well, *I* must say you're going to have to be patient! How do you suppose we're ever going to get to the top? It's a very long way to climb.'

As they peered up at it, silhouetted against the brilliant sky, the Doctor became aware of a strange, high-pitched whistling sound. It seemed to be coming closer and closer – like a giant mosquito – or a shell fired from a cannon – or –

'Look out!' he shouted suddenly. '*Duck*, Zoe!'

They threw themselves flat upon the stony ground, and the missile – whatever it might have been – passed harmlessly over them, before exploding in a lurid flash of searing white light against the cliff face.

A cloud of dust enveloped them for an instant, then slowly began to fade, leaving them choking and spluttering.

'Whatever was that?' Zoe gasped.

'I haven't the faintest idea . . . Except that it seemed to be aimed at us – and rather too accurately for my liking!'

Zoe lifted her head, wiping the dust and grime from her face with the back of her hand, and said in an apprehensive whisper: 'Doctor . . . When that thing exploded against the rock – am I imagining it, or did you see a *word* in the middle of the explosion? As it flared up like a bolt of lightning – in the middle of it, in a sort of star-shape, I thought I saw the word *BOOM* . . . Did you see it too?'

'Thank heavens – I thought I must be going a little crazy,' the Doctor agreed gratefully. 'Yes – *BOOM* – in capital letters, and with an exclamation mark after it . . . What can it mean?'

As if in answer to his question, they both heard a sudden, ear-splitting shout – like a war-cry: a wordless yell of hatred. But the strange part was – at the same moment, they both saw a balloon float up above the rocks: and the balloon contained the single word: *YARGHRROO!*

'It's no language I ever came across before – and yet it seems vaguely familiar.' The Doctor pondered this little puzzle. 'But where are these words and non-words coming from?'

A sudden rattle of loose stones alerted them, and they swung around to find they were no longer alone.

The figure that confronted them was an awesome sight. For one thing, he was a giant of a man: a towering Hercules, with bulging muscles, which looked all the more remarkable since they were outlined upon his torso in a spider's web of deep purple lines . . . And his skin was bright green.

By way of clothing, he wore a pair of shining purple tights and thigh-length silver boots: around his naked, massive shoulders there swirled a black silk cape, and on his bullet head he wore a black skull cap and a half-mask. And in his hands he carried a very extraordinary ray gun, made of glittering plastic and metal.

Zoe gave a cry – whether of fear or of recognition, it was hard to tell – and exclaimed: 'The Karkus!'

Strangest of all, the man stood posed and motionless for a few seconds, as if frozen to the spot, then he announced in a thick, guttural accent: 'You . . . are . . . my . . . prisoners.'

'That remains to be seen,' said the Doctor, trying to appear casual. 'But first perhaps you should introduce yourself, my good man. Who are you?'

'I . . . am . . . the . . . Karkus,' came the reply, in the same thick, metallic voice.

'I told you, he's the Karkus,' Zoe hissed urgently, in the Doctor's ear. 'Spelled K-A-R-K-U-S – and pronounced "carcase", on account of his physique . . . Don't ever let him get you in a hammerlock.'

'I wouldn't dream of it – dear me, now what is the fellow playing at?'

For on the word 'hammerlock', the newcomer had suddenly changed his position, adopting an even more menacing stance, and pointing the ray gun at the Doctor's head.

'Raise . . . your . . . hands . . . above . . . your . . . head,' the grating tones went on. 'Obey . . . or . . . I . . . fire!'

'That pea-shooter?' The Doctor laughed gently. 'Forgive me – but what kind of weapon is that supposed to be?'

Zoe said urgently: 'That's his anti-molecular ray disintegrator – he never goes anywhere without it.'

'Stuff and nonsense,' said the Doctor. 'Anti-molecular, my left foot – such a weapon is scientifically impossible – it doesn't exist.'

And as if to prove his point, as he said these words, there was a sharp *ping*, and the ray gun abruptly disappeared.

(As it vanished, they noticed that the word *PING!* materialised for a moment between the Karkus's empty hands.)

The Karkus discovered that he was unarmed and froze again, clenching his fists in a very threatening manner, and uttering a fearful guttural noise at the back of his throat.

(Above his head floated the word *GHRRRGH!*)

'An interesting spelling,' said the Doctor, 'but not, I fancy, to be found in the Oxford Dictionary.'

'I . . . tear . . . you . . . limb . . . from . . . limb!' articulated the Karkus, with some difficulty.

'Oh, Doctor, please be careful - he could do it, you see - the Karkus has superhuman strength . . . Try not to annoy him.'

'Annoy him? My dear girl, I never saw him before in my life, why should I want to annoy *him*? He's beginning to annoy *me* with his sub-human manners and his lack of civilised conversation . . .'

Before he could finish, the Doctor found himself being grasped by two colossal hands, each one as big as a leg of mutton, only bright green. The Karkus lifted him several feet off the ground, and Zoe screamed: 'Take care, Doctor - remember he's only a fictional character too - say you don't believe in him - '

The Doctor exclaimed irritably and a little breathlessly, from his uncomfortable position in mid-air: 'Believe in him? I don't believe or disbelieve - how can I? I never even heard of him till now - my dear fellow, kindly put me down!'

The Karkus gave another terrifying cry (*YEEIKE!*) and dumped the Doctor unceremoniously on the ground. (*SPLAT!*) Then he seemed as if he were about to jump upon him like an all-in-wrestler - but he was distracted at the last moment by Zoe, who walked up to him with a polite smile, and one hand outstretched, saying: 'How do you do? My name's Zoe - so nice to meet you.'

The Karkus turned - as jerkily as before - to face her, with a puzzled green frown beetling his brows. The Doctor struggled to his feet, calling out: 'Zoe - have you gone mad? What are you doing?'

'Lesson Seventeen, from Basic Course in Self-Preservation - I learned this at Mind-Training School,' said Zoe airily.

Then everything seemed to happen at once: the Karkus grabbed her hand, and Zoe threw her weight sideways and downwards - and amazingly the mighty creature suddenly flew through the air, grunting with pain as he hit the rocky floor. (*UH!*)

He quickly recovered, picked himself up, and made another, murderous attack upon Zoe, who muttered, 'Lesson Eighteen B,' and sidestepped.

She gave another expert flick of her wrist, and he fell the other way this time. (*OUCH!*)

The Doctor tried to go to Zoe's assistance – but she seemed to be managing very well without him. As the Karkus made one last assault Zoe countered with a throw that sent him flying, head over heels, landing flat on his back.

At once, she put her foot under his chin – hard – and remarked: 'You'd better give up, you know. The carotid artery can only take a certain amount of pressure.'

'Mercy . . . Mercy!' grunted the Karkus.

'Do you submit?' asked Zoe.

He slapped his hand flat on the ground: and she lifted her foot.

'That's more like it,' she said cheerfully. 'And don't be so silly another time, there's a good boy.'

The Karkus dragged himself painfully to his feet, saying: 'I . . . am . . . your . . . slave . . . Command . . . me.'

Zoe turned to the Doctor: 'We may as well get him to help us – he's not a bad lad, at heart – in fact, as long as he's on the right side, he can be a tower of strength.' To the Karkus, she said, 'Do you know the best way to get to the Citadel?'

'I . . . know . . . it . . .'

'Then take us there – as soon as possible.'

The Karkus had lost his black silk cape in the struggle, and now he set off among the rocks without it. The Doctor automatically picked it up and put it on: it seemed the easiest way to carry it. As the muscleman disappeared into the distance, he asked quietly: 'Who did you say this chap is – exactly? You mentioned a fictional character, but I'm afraid I can't quite place him . . .'

'Oh, you *must* know the Karkus!' exclaimed Zoe. 'We all follow his adventures at home – in the strip section of the *Hourly Telepress*.'

'Strip section? Ah, that explains it!' Light dawned, and

the Doctor's face broke into a smile. 'He's a character from the comic strips of the year 2000 . . . That accounts for all those amazing words and balloons – and the way he kept freezing into one position after another – I see it all now . . . Only I'm afraid I never heard of him.'

'But surely – you've been in the year 2000 – '

'Ah, yes, indeed – a nice place to visit, but I wouldn't want to live there . . . and quite frankly, I was rather preoccupied with other matters at the time . . . I had very little opportunity to follow the comic strips.'

'Well, we'd better start following *this* one!' Zoe advised him: 'He must be halfway up the cliff by now!'

The comic strip giant may not have had a great deal of intelligence in his granite skull, but he certainly knew the best way to climb up to the Citadel. And though he had a physique like a lumbering ox, it was quite surprising to find that he could move as lightly as any gazelle when the need arose.

Now he led the way up a narrow track, littered with fallen stones, picking his way confidently between one boulder and the next. Zoe and the Doctor did their best to catch up with him – but he had a head start, and it wasn't easy.

The track zig-zagged back and forth along the lower slopes of the cliff face, and then took an unexpected turn and burrowed under a natural arch in the rock, disappearing for a few yards, and then appearing again around the side of the escarpment.

Here, the going was rougher, and the path became steeper: then it turned another corner, and suddenly, dramatically, transformed itself into a flight of stone steps, that led upward – on and on – as if they would reach out and touch the sky.

The Doctor and Zoe had long since stopped talking: they needed all their breath for a climb like this! Now they exchanged unhappy glances, and soldiered on, up those never-ending steps . . .

It seemed as if they would never reach their goal, but at long last, breathless and groaning, they found themselves on a narrow terrace, fringed by a stone balustrade, and there, facing them, was an imposing pair of oaken doors, flanked by two sturdy pillars.

The Karkus, who was not at all out of breath, bowed obsequiously to Zoe, and indicated the old fashioned iron bell-pull beside the double doors.

'Oh – ah – thank you . . . Very much,' panted Zoe.

'Yes – thanks – my dear – er – ' The Doctor whispered in Zoe's ear: 'What did you say his name was?'

'Karkus. K-A-R-K-U-S . . . '

'Yes, quite absurd, of course – but nevertheless . . . Thank you, Mr Karkus, I don't think we need trouble you any further.'

Zoe added: 'That's right – we shan't be requiring you any more. You can run along now.'

'I . . . obey . . . ' said the Karkus: and with one last, low bow he took his leave of them, shambling off along the terrace, and out of sight around the corner.

The Doctor mopped his brow absent-mindedly with the corner of the black silk cape – and realised belatedly what he was wearing.

'Oh – how very tiresome – the poor fellow's gone off without his cloak – oh, well, it's too late to call him back now. And you never can tell – it might come in handy! . . . Let's go.'

He advanced towards the bell-push, but Zoe tugged at his arm. 'What are you doing? We can't just ring the bell and walk in!'

'Why ever not?' retorted the Doctor. 'It's the usual method. I don't have any calling cards to leave, unfortunately, but I'm sure that our host will overlook that, under the circumstances.'

'You mean you're going to tell the Master who we are – and expect him to invite us in for a nice, cosy cup of tea?'

'Not quite that, my dear . . . I'm not quite as green as – as your friend, Mr Karkus! I'm well aware that we are in a world of fiction: so we must announce ourselves accordingly.

Now then – if I might suggest that you make yourself scarce for a moment . . . ?'

He held out the voluminous cape, flinging it around Zoe's shoulders, and drawing her close to him so that she was completely hidden.

From the depths of the cloak, her voice sounded muffled and uncertain: 'Are you really sure this is a good idea?'

By way of reply, the Doctor pulled the bell: and they both heard the sonorous clanging of an old-fashioned bell as it pealed somewhere within the building. For a few seconds, nothing happened: and then a small metal grille slid open in one of the wooden door-panels, and a harsh voice demanded: 'State your name and attribution.'

The Doctor took a deep breath, then replied in a passable impersonation of the comic-strip character: 'I . . . am . . . the . . . Karkus.'

'And your attribution?'

('What's that?' whispered Zoe – but the Doctor silenced her swiftly.)

'From . . . year . . . 2000 . . . Comic . . . strip . . . in . . . *Hourly . . . Telepress*.'

There was another short wait, and then the voice responded: 'Authenticated . . . You may enter the Citadel.'

The grille slid shut, and the huge wooden doors swung open. The Doctor walked forward, into the darkness of the entrance hall, with Zoe still concealed beneath his cloak.

With a reverberating thud that sounded horribly final, the double doors closed behind them: and then there was the sound of a lock clanging shut, and of bolts grinding into place.

At the Control Centre, the Master – who had been watching this little charade through a television camera concealed in the door panel – sat back in his chair, and smiled with satisfaction.

'Mission accomplished,' he said happily. 'This time, the trap was foolproof.'

112

8

A Meeting of Masters

'I wish I could make you understand!' exclaimed Jamie, in a sudden burst of frustration.

He paced the word-processing laboratory in which he was still trapped, desperately trying to find some way to get through to Lemuel Gulliver. For his part, Gulliver sat patiently on top of the storage cupboard, swinging his stockinged legs and trying to fathom what Jamie was talking about.

'You still say you saw no-one and heard nothing when the White Robots entered this room?' Jamie continued.

'I know not what they mean,' repeated Gulliver.

Jamie sighed, and tackled the problem from another angle. 'Listen . . . You heard the voice giving orders to search for me . . . Why do you suppose that happened?'

Gulliver shrugged. 'I conjecture that these were orders given by some person in authority.'

'The Master?'

The traveller hesitated for a moment, then replied cautiously: 'It is possible.'

'All right then . . . If there aren't any robots – whose job is it to carry out these orders? Who was I hiding from?'

'Why, sir, the Yahoos – without doubt.'

Now it was Jamie's turn to be at a loss. 'What do you mean by Yahoos? Who are they?'

'A cursed race of inferior creatures – I never beheld so disagreeable an animal.'

They looked at each other blankly: the chasm of misunderstanding between them was wider and deeper than ever.

Jamie threw up his hands in despair. 'This isn't getting us anywhere, is it? I've never seen any Yahoos, and you've never seen any White Robots, so we don't know what we're both talking about . . .'

Then he looked round swiftly, at the sound of the door opening, alert to defend himself. But in the open doorway – to his immense relief – stood not an enemy, but two friends: the people he most wanted to see.

'Doctor! Zoe!'

'Jamie – at last – '

Zoe took a step forward, but Jamie warned her not to come any closer.

'Stay where you are! Don't move!'

'What's the matter?' she asked.

'There's some sort of gadget hidden down there – a kind of light, and if you walk through it you'll set off the alarm system. I got it going myself when I tried to get out – that's why they sent a gang of White Robots to hunt me down.'

'White Robots – here? Like the ones we met before?' asked Zoe in dismay.

'Aye, the very same.'

'Doctor, did you hear that?'

But the Doctor was hardly listening: he was much more interested in the warning system, and had stooped down to examine the beam of light.

'Ah, yes, the Robots. I'm not surprised, I thought they'd turn up sooner or later . . . But *this* is really fascinating – an early twentieth-century device based upon a simple photo-electric cell. Just make sure you step over it, Zoe, without breaking the circuit – like this . . . '

He led the way, high-stepping across the light-ray; and no alarm bells sounded. Zoe followed his example, while Jamie watched apprehensively: but all was well.

She hugged him with relief, and kissed him on the cheek. 'Thank goodness you're safe and sound – what happened in the labyrinth? When we got back, you'd disappeared – though we did find your jacket.'

Now the Doctor returned the rough tweed coat, and Jamie slipped it on, thankfully, as he explained: 'Well, I had one of those tin soldiers hot on my heels. But luckily I was able to do a bit of rock-climbing, and I got myself up the cliff face – robots can't climb, you see . . . But now I'm here, I'm not

114

too sure how I'm going to get out again. I hid from the White Robots when they came searching for me, though this gentleman still refuses to believe it – '

'I know not what they mean,' repeated Gulliver, doggedly.

'Don't start all that again! At least we're all together now – so let's make some sort of plan to get out of here.'

The Doctor shook his head: 'Sorry – I'm not leaving yet . . . I only just got here! Besides, I have some important business to attend to.'

Zoe chimed in: 'The Doctor's made up his mind – he's going to see the Master.'

For the first time, Lemuel Gulliver looked alarmed. He stood up and rubbed his chin, saying uneasily: 'This resolution, perhaps, may appear very bold and dangerous.'

Zoe said: 'I couldn't agree more – that's exactly what I keep telling him, but he won't listen to me.'

'What makes you say that?' the Doctor asked Gulliver.

'I think you should not be here. The Master makes the rules for the government of this Kingdom: it would be unwise for you to disobey.'

'You think he shouldn't try to see the Master?' said Zoe. 'So do I.'

Gulliver pondered, then said: 'If you will consider my advice . . . Swear a peace with him and his Kingdom: find yourselves a place to lodge, and stay quietly – with the expectation that things would mend.'

The Doctor nodded, and appeared to take this recommendation to heart. 'Yes – I see . . . Well, I shall certainly think over your advice very carefully, my dear chap . . . I'm sure we're all very grateful.'

Gulliver doffed his hat and bowed low: 'Your servant, sir . . . Young lady – and young gentleman . . . Your servant.'

And he took his leave of them – passing through the electric beam once more without disturbing it in the very least. The door shut behind him.

'But if you don't see the Master, what will you do?' Jamie wanted to know.

'Who says I won't see the Master? It's what I came to do! I can be rather stubborn, once my mind is made up.'

'But Doctor – ' Zoe protested. 'You told Mr Gulliver you'd take his advice and – '

'Forgive me, my dear – I told him I would *think* about his advice. Well, now I've thought – and I'm quite convinced I'm doing the right thing. We've got to fight back – take the battle into the enemy camp.'

'That's more like it!' Jamie rubbed his hands. 'What's the matter, Zoe – are you feeling scared?'

'I'm not scared exactly – ' she hedged. 'But I do think it's all pretty hopeless . . . I mean, we're surrounded and out-numbered – we're fighting in the dark – we never know where the next attack is coming from . . . The Medusa was bad enough, but – '

'Oh, aye – the Medusa,' Jamie remembered. 'I read about that – while I was here.'

'You *read* about it?' The Doctor cocked an enquiring eyebrow. 'How? Where?'

Jamie crossed to the ticker-tape machine, picked up a handful of paper ribbon and showed it to the Doctor.

'See for yourself . . . This stuff kept churning out – and then it suddenly stopped.'

'*The Doctor test report . . . Failure . . . Cancel . . .*' The Doctor frowned, and slowly his brain cleared. 'Do you know, I believe I'm beginning to understand.'

'I wish I did,' said Jamie ruefully.

'Look at it this way,' the Doctor began, taking it step by step. 'When someone writes about an incident that has actually happened – we call it history . . . You follow me so far?'

'Aye – go on.'

'But suppose someone writes about something that hasn't really happened – we call it fiction – right?'

'Right.'

'So if the written word comes first, and the incident happens after it – this is how fiction is created. The Master wrote about a sword, tempting me to slay the Medusa. If I'd

116

fallen into the trap and actually done it – suiting the action to the word, so to speak – it would have become an incident in fiction, and I myself would have turned into a fictional character!'

'That's horrible . . . ' Zoe shuddered. 'What would have happened to you after that?'

'After that – I should only have been able to say or do whatever the Master created for me to say and do . . . I should have been trapped in this dimension for ever – a figment of his imagination.'

'Trapped for ever – ?' Zoe shied away. 'Come on, let's get out of here – before it's too late!'

'Zoe, *be careful* – !'

The Doctor tried to call her back, but it all happened so quickly – she stepped through the beam of light, saying: 'It must be safe – Mr Gulliver walked through it – '

And as she broke the circuit, all the alarm bells began jangling again, and the metallic, distorted voice boomed through the speakers: 'Attention, attention! There are still aliens at large . . . Renew the search . . . '

Zoe retreated in horror: 'I'm sorry – I didn't realise – I thought if he went through – '

The Doctor explained: 'Gulliver isn't real, remember – he's not flesh and blood like us.'

'That's true,' Jamie agreed. 'I noticed myself – he doesn't cast any shadow.' Then he broke off, hearing the approaching electronic hum. 'The Robots – they're on their way . . . There won't be room for all of us in yon wee cupboard!'

'Where else can we hide?' Zoe looked around frantically.

Only the Doctor stood his ground: curiously unmoved. 'We don't need a hiding-place,' he said calmly.

'What do you mean? We can't let them find us – '

'That is exactly what I mean to do . . . Let them find us.'

Jamie exclaimed in dismay: 'You mean – just stay here – and wait for them to round us up like sheep?'

'Why not? We shall ask – very politely – for an interview with the Master.'

Zoe said unhappily: 'What makes you think they'll give us

time to ask anything at all? They may believe that actions speak louder than words!'

And then her words died upon her lips – for the door opened once more, and three White Robots advanced into the room. They lined up, facing the three time-travellers – and the circular compound lenses which they carried began to glow with a dazzling light: at the same time, a high-pitched bleeping arose above the continuing electronic sound – urgent and menacing.

The Doctor enquired, as nonchalantly as possible: 'Are you looking for us, by any chance?'

There was a long pause, during which the lenses threw out an even more blinding light, and the bleeping reached a shrill crescendo. Zoe put her hands to her ears.

'Very well!' the Doctor continued, raising his voice above the din. 'In that case I have only one thing to say to you . . . *I demand to see the Master*!'

At the sound of the Master's name, the Robots seemed to retreat slightly, and the lights were extinguished immediately. The noise stopped, and for a few seconds there was complete silence – until a low rumbling drew their attention to the wall at the far end of the room.

An entire panel slid back to reveal pitch blackness beyond. It was through this same hidden panel that Jamie had seen the last platoon of robots disappearing, some time earlier.

'Do you suppose we're meant to go through there?' he asked.

No-one spoke, and no-one moved. The three White Robots stood like statues, cutting off the only other way out of the room.

'It rather seems so,' said the Doctor. 'I wonder if the Master is a creature of nocturnal habits? He appears to live in total darkness.'

Zoe felt a chill run down her spine – for the response to the Doctor's little joke was unexpected and somehow terrifying. A jovial chuckle emanated from the darkness, and a voice cried in welcoming tones: 'Aha – that's very droll – I must

118

remember that . . . A nocturnal animal, indeed! . . . Do come in, my dear Doctor – I've been expecting you.'

The Doctor took a long breath: this was the moment he had been waiting for. Zoe felt for Jamie's hand, and clutched it.

The voice continued genially: 'Please don't be alarmed . . . Won't you step into my parlour?'

'Said the spider to the fly . . . ' The Doctor completed the couplet, and threw a grin to his companions which was meant to be reassuring. 'Come on – it would be churlish to keep our host waiting.'

He set off boldly into the open doorway, and the other two followed him.

The darkness was so thick it seemed to enfold them physically, like a blanket. Zoe felt it muffling her from head to foot – eyes, ears, all her senses completely swathed in that total, terrifying blackness.

Ahead, the Doctor cleared his throat and ventured: 'It is a little difficult to – um – see one's way . . . Where are you, sir?'

'Here . . . Where I have always been . . . Waiting to meet you,' said the voice, now a good deal nearer.

And then they moved from the fog of darkness into a pool of light – and Zoe gasped. The Master was not at all what she had been expecting.

He sat in a high-backed chair with the control desk in front of him, and the bank of television monitor screens to one side. Behind him, a whole wall of computer equipment purred, blinked and flashed as spools revolved, stopped and rewound in meaningless patterns.

Somehow the Master seemed out of place amidst these highly technological surroundings – for he was a dear little old gentleman: benignly smiling, white-haired, clad in an old dressing-gown and a skullcap, with half-moon spectacles askew on the end of his pudgy round nose.

He held out the hand of friendship, saying: 'Doctor – this is a great pleasure . . . And your two young companions – now, let me see . . . '

He consulted an open file on his desk: 'Ah, yes – Zoe and Jamie – quite so . . . I have your dossiers in front of me.'

'You appear to be very well organised, if I may say so.' The Doctor spoke casually but his mind was racing; without appearing to do so, his eyes were flashing glances to left and right, searching for clues concerning the function of this bizarre establishment.

The Master acknowledged the compliment with a modest nod of his head: 'Oh, yes, indeed – but then we have to be . . . The running of this place requires enormous attention to detail. It's a responsible position that I hold, but very rewarding.'

He was, the Doctor realised, more than a little vain. And what were those two slim wires which seemed to grow out of his skullcap?

'Responsible – I'm sure you are,' the Doctor continued pleasantly. 'But responsible to whom? To someone else in authority?'

'Not to some*one*,' the Master corrected him. 'I take instruction from a higher power – higher than any you could begin to imagine . . . Although I must not underestimate your amazing imaginative ability, Doctor – and I really must congratulate you on the great skill with which you tackled the various stages of your examination.'

'Well, I soon realised I was being put to the test – but the problem was to find out the purpose *behind* all those tests. I couldn't make head or tail of that.'

The Master chuckled again, rubbing his hands sympathetically: 'I know, I know – when I was first brought here myself, I was just as bewildered as you are now!'

Jamie ventured to ask: 'How long have you been here, sir?'

The Master's eyes grew mistily reminiscent: 'I left England in the summer of 1926 . . . It was a very hot day, I remember – I think I must have dozed off over my desk – and when I awoke . . . Ah, but that's a long story . . . And talking of long stories – did you ever hear of the Adventures of Captain Jack Harkaway?'

Zoe and Jamie looked blankly at one another, and Zoe said politely: 'I'm afraid not . . . Have you heard of him, Doctor?'

The Doctor appeared to be lost in thought: he had been trying to see where those two leads were attached. They seemed to be connected to the bank of computers, behind the Master's desk – or rather to the strange abstract object that stood at the heart of the computer display . . . A huge, whirled shape, imprisoned in a glass case: patterned like coral, and shaped like the kernel of a walnut, it pulsed with an inner light – now white, now gleaming with a deep rose . . . What could it be?

Jamie tugged at the Doctor's sleeve: 'Hey, Doctor – Captain Jack Harkaway – have you heard of him?'

'What? Oh, I beg your pardon – I was daydreaming . . . Harkaway? – wait a moment – wasn't he a character in a serial? I seem to remember it appeared in a schoolboy magazine – '

The Master looked highly gratified: 'Too kind, too kind, my dear sir . . . The magazine was *The Ensign* – and for twenty-five years I delivered five thousand words every week.'

'So you're a writer!' Jamie exclaimed, and Zoe – using her phenomenal mathematical talent – made a rapid calculation: 'Twenty-five years – five thousand words every week – that's well over six million words!'

'It was probably some kind of a record, I dare say,' smiled the Master. 'Anyway, that is why I was selected to take charge here.'

Jamie looked around: 'You're in charge of all *this*?'

'In one sense, I am.'

Suddenly the Doctor recognised that complex coral-like shape – it was a gigantic brain . . . And the leads from the Master's head led straight into it.

'Might it not be more accurate to say that all this – these computers, this equipment – is in charge of *you*?' he enquired.

The Master's smile grew chilly, and his eyes were no

longer friendly as he stared back over his half-moon glasses.

'Not at all,' he said flatly. 'They couldn't do without me . . . My creative genius is the source of power that keeps this whole operation going. I am at the very centre of the organisation.'

'So I see,' said the Doctor. 'And you are virtually a prisoner – isn't that right?'

The Master drew himself up indignantly and began: 'I have sole charge of – '

But before he could complete the sentence, the giant brain changed colour once more, through crimson to a throbbing mauve: and all the computers began whirring and clicking away busily. The Master closed his eyes for a second, as if fighting off an overpowering headache, and then said with an effort: 'You must excuse me for a moment . . . '

He picked up his pen and began to write in the open book that lay on the desk in front of him, totally absorbed in his task.

Jamie and Zoe edged closer to the Doctor, and Jamie whispered: 'Come on, Doctor – let's get out of here – I've had enough of this place.'

And Zoe urged: 'Yes, let's – there's something going on here that gives me the creeps!'

The Doctor shook his head: 'I can't leave yet – I need to know more.'

'Aye, well – you keep the old fellow talking,' said Jamie, 'while Zoe and me try to find a way out. Look at all those alleyways – they must lead somewhere . . . '

Now that their eyes had grown accustomed to this twilight world, illuminated entirely by the great brain, they could see that they were in the centre of a colossal library. From the control-desk at the centre, alleys ran off in all directions like the spokes of a wheel, each one lined with bookshelves – shelves stacked so high that their tops could not be seen: they ran up into darkness and disappeared.

Now the light changed once again, and the busy

computers halted their frantic activity. The Master put down his pen and smiled: 'So sorry to have deserted you – but needs must . . . Now – where had I got to?'

The Doctor remarked: 'I hope you were about to answer my question . . . Are you a prisoner here?'

He stepped closer to the desk, and at the same moment Jamie and Zoe slipped back into the shadows. They hoped that the Master would be so fascinated by this discussion, that he might not even notice them creeping out. From the corner of his eye, the Master noticed and pursed his lips in satisfaction, as he continued his conversation with the Doctor.

'I wouldn't put it quite like that. I am extremely happy here – I have everything I could possibly want – this amazing library, with every known work of fiction – all the master-pieces written by Earthlings since the beginning of time . . . '

His voice faded as Zoe and Jamie drew further off, out of sight behind the endless walls of books.

'I don't think he saw us,' whispered Zoe.

'Let's hope not,' said Jamie. 'Come on, take a look along here and see if we can find a way of escape.'

The Doctor too was aware of their departure, and he too pretended that he hadn't seen them go. Playing for time, he continued: 'I begin to understand at last . . . Of course, only the human race has the power to create fiction – the power to imagine.'

'Exactly,' the Master concurred. 'This is one field in which the intelligence that I serve cannot compete. They need man – a man, of boundless imagination – as a power-house . . . Which is why they selected me, all those years ago.'

'But that still doesn't explain why I have been brought here,' the Doctor cut in. 'And just what is this intelligence – this higher power you speak of? What does it want with me?'

The Master shrugged, and spread his hands wide:

'As you see – I am no longer young. Whereas you, my dear Doctor, are timeless. You exist outside the barriers of space and time: therefore you are the perfect choice to replace me . . . To take over my post – in this unique situation.'

'So that's it . . . ' The Doctor folded his arms. 'You should have said so in the first place – it would have saved us both a lot of trouble. Because my answer is no!'

'You refuse?'

'Emphatically!'

The computers began to whirr again, insistently and angrily: lights flashed, and the imprisoned brain darkened from mauve to purple. The Master's face was not benign now: his expression became threatening and inhuman.

'Refusal is impossible,' he said – and the Doctor recognised the clipped metallic tones of the voice he had heard issuing orders over the loudspeakers: 'You are here to serve us . . . There is no alternative!'

Zoe and Jamie, still searching through the library, were lost in a spider's-web of alleys that led nowhere.

'There's got to be a way out,' Zoe repeated desperately.

'Of course! There must be another door somewhere,' agreed Jamie. 'If we can get the Doctor away before – '

They turned another corner, and stopped dead in their tracks. They were face to face with one of the White Robots.

'Quick! Run for it!' Jamie exclaimed. 'Back the way we came – '

'*Jamie – Look out!*' cried Zoe.

For there, immediately behind them, were two more White Robots, cutting off their retreat. There was no escape.

In the soulless, computer voice, the Master continued: 'Resistance is useless . . . Submit your will for the sake of a greater good . . . It has been decided.'

'That is something I prefer to decide for myself,' retorted the Doctor.

The computer clicked off, and the lights came up again to a normal level. Instantly, the Master returned to his old self, affable and ingratiating – but now the affability was false and unreliable, and his friendliness could not be trusted.

'My dear sir,' he continued blandly; 'I think you will find there is only one decision open to you . . . Why fight against it? You are clearly destined to take over my task – you and I are the only two beings in the Universe who could tackle it . . . I realised the moment I set eyes on you – we are both Masters, in our own way.'

'Your way is not mine,' said the Doctor stubbornly. 'I shall never agree.'

'Of your own accord – perhaps not . . . But with a little persuasion you might change your mind.' The Master gestured to the open book before him, and read aloud the sentences he had just been writing: *'Jamie and Zoe attempted to escape, but on making off through the library, they were ambushed by a party of robot guards, and overpowered . . .'*

The Doctor looked round anxiously: 'No! It's another trick – Zoe ! Where are you?'

By way of reply, the Master switched on the television screens: they all showed an identical picture.

Zoe and Jamie were being forced back by the troop of White Robots – back to what seemed to be two white walls . . . But the walls had words upon them, and the Doctor realised that they were the pages of an enormous book. The Robots pressed in from either side, and began to push the covers shut. The Doctor saw Zoe open her mouth to scream for help, but he could hear nothing. All he could do was watch – helplessly – as the mighty book began to close, and Zoe and Jamie were slowly trapped between its pages . . . Caught for ever in the dimension of fiction . . .

'Now, then,' continued the Master, looking over his spectacles, 'are you prepared to co-operate? Your life – in return for theirs? Is it a bargain?'

9

Lives in the Balance

'Your life – in return for theirs?' The Master repeated his offer. 'Well – which is it to be?'

'You can't kill them!' the Doctor protested. 'You're a human being – you couldn't be so heartless!'

The Master smiled and shook his head, then indicated the banks of TV screens. They all showed the same picture: the gigantic book had now been firmly closed, and on its spine, the Doctor could read the title: *The Story of Jamie and Zoe.*

'They're neither dead nor alive,' the Master explained, taking off his spectacles and rubbing his eyes. 'They're no longer human beings either – merely fictional characters. *But* – ' he paused, dramatically.

'But what?'

'But they could be released, and revert to their former status . . . If you consent to take my place.'

'You would really do that?' the Doctor asked, suspiciously.

'No, no, my dear sir, – *you* would. That's the whole point.' He breathed on his glasses and began to polish them carefully with his handkerchief. 'You see – once you take up your new post, it will be your first official task, as the new Master.'

The Doctor looked suddenly very tired. 'I see,' he said, in a voice drained of all emotion. 'So that's your scheme . . . Very ingenious . . . I congratulate you.'

The old man purred with satisfaction: 'I take it you do agree?'

But the Doctor squared his shoulders and replied: 'I'm sorry . . . My answer is still no . . . And now if you will excuse me – '

He turned to walk away – and found that the White Robots were advancing upon him. He looked quickly to left and right, and saw that down every aisle of this vast library, more and more Robots were moving steadily towards him.

The Master said, with an edge of steel in his tone: 'I shall be sorry to have to use violent methods, but you must submit. You have no alternative.'

The Doctor glanced around desperately: realising that he was cornered. But if all the ways of escape at ground level were barred to him – there was still another way he could go: upwards!

He moved swiftly to the nearest wall of bookshelves, and began to shin up them, using each shelf as the rung of a ladder, and exclaiming: 'Jamie was right – I have yet to meet a Robot who can climb!'

Hand over hand he pulled himself up into the darkness at the top of the shelves, and disappeared from view.

Oddly enough, the Master did not make the least attempt to stop him. He did not even appear to be disturbed by the Doctor's rapid exit. Replacing the spectacles on the end of his button nose, he said with quiet confidence: 'Very well – we will play this game of hide and seek a little longer . . . The Doctor cannot possibly escape.'

And the newly-polished lenses in their half-moon frames gleamed with a sinister light.

The Doctor climbed on through the dusty, cobwebbed shadows at the top of the bookshelves, and at last found an ancient ventilator shaft. He could smell fresh air – cool and sweet, after the stuffy enclosed space of the library. He pulled himself into the shaft, head first, and struggled upwards like one of the small boys that chimney sweeps used to employ in the olden days: hoping – as the boys must have hoped with all their hearts – that he would not get stuck.

After a few nasty moments, he found himself clambering out on to the roof of the citadel. Night had fallen, and now he looked up at the black velvet sky with tiny stars scattered across it like diamond dust.

All around him were the fairy tale towers, domes and pinnacles of the fantastic castle, rising up from a flat, tiled roof. He walked to the edge, and looked over the crenellated battlements . . . Even in the darkness, he could tell that he was staring down into a sheer drop . . . No escape that way, clearly.

He set off on an expedition round the roof – and stopped short, flattening himself against the edge of a tower, as footsteps approached . . . Then, with a sigh of relief, he left his hiding-place . . .

'Zoe – Jamie – at last! Thank goodness I've found you.'

The two youngsters smiled politely, and Jamie said: 'Doctor! I'm certainly glad to see you again.'

'Yes, indeed – it's a great relief,' the Doctor agreed. 'The Master tried to tell me that you were both – '

But they didn't seem to hear what he said, and interrupted him, talking to one another.

'Well, where do we go from here?' Jamie asked.

'Back to the TARDIS,' said Zoe.

'No, we can't,' said Jamie. 'It fell apart, don't you remember?'

'Well, it's over now, thank goodness,' said Zoe. 'I want to sit and rest for a while.'

'The TARDIS broke up – it fell apart, don't you remember?' asked Jamie.

'Yes, I know – you told me about that . . . ' The Doctor tried to interject, but they weren't even looking at him. 'What's wrong with you both?'

'Well, where do we go from here?' asked Jamie eagerly.

'Back to the TARDIS?' suggested Zoe.

'No, we can't – it fell apart, don't you remember?' retorted Jamie.

The Doctor went up to them, with a horrid realisation dawning upon him . . . They kept saying the same things, over and over again . . . He snapped his fingers in Jamie's face: Jamie didn't even blink, but remarked tonelessly: 'I've been in a fog – no, I mean *really* in a fog – ever since the TARDIS broke up.'

The Doctor remembered him uttering the self-same phrases when they first found one another in the forest of words . . . So the Master's threat had been carried out: they were no longer human beings – simply fictitious creatures, doomed to repeat the same speeches again and again.

He turned away, unable to look at them: two-dimensional replicas of his dear friends. With a heavy heart, he found himself gazing down through a glass skylight into the room below – and recognized it as the word-processing laboratory. As he watched, the teleprinter clattered out a stream of paper ribbon. Straining his eyes, he could just make out the words: ' . . . *ambushed by a party of roboi guards and over-powered* . . . '

So that must be the master tape. He tried to think constructively: 'I wonder . . . Perhaps – if I were to create a few immortal words of fiction myself, I might give the story a happier ending?'

He looked back toward Jamie and Zoe, who stood as he left them, still quietly repeating their stereotyped conversation: and he made up his mind. *Anything* was worth trying.

He tried to open the skylight – but the huge pane of glass in its thick wooden frame was far too heavy for him to shift by himself. He strained to move it but it wouldn't budge.

'This is hopeless,' he muttered breathlessly. 'What I need is the strength of the Karkus . . . '

At once there was a lurid flash, and the green muscleman appeared by his side, grunting: 'I . . . am . . . at . . . your . . . command.'

'Oh! Well, that's extremely obliging of you. I wonder, could you lift this window frame for me, my dear fellow?'

The Karkus raised it without the slightest effort, pulling it off its hinges, and holding it high above his head, enquiring: 'This . . . is . . . what . . . you . . . want?'

'Ah – well, I don't actually *want* it . . . Just get rid of it, will you?'

Obediently, the Karkus tossed a huge piece of glass over the battlements, and the Doctor heard a distant crash a few seconds later as it shattered on the rocks, far below.

'Thank you so much,' he said. 'Now, all I have to do is to

get down into that room somehow . . . It's too far to jump – I really need some sort of – '

Another flash – and the Princess Rapunzel was standing beside the Karkus, holding out her long plait of blonde hair, and saying: 'A rope? Allow me.'

She let the plait drop through the open skylight. The Doctor blinked at her doubtfully: 'Your Royal Highness – I take it you must be the Princess Rapunzel – but are you quite sure?'

She sighed, and said: 'Please – everyone else uses it, for climbing up and down – I don't see why you shouldn't . . . I suppose you're not a prince, by any chance?'

'I'm awfully sorry to disappoint you, no, I'm not . . . '
The Doctor swung his leg over the edge of the frame and added consolingly: 'Never mind, your Highness – some day your prince will come – to coin a phrase . . . Now, if you could very kindly take the strain?' And using the rope of hair, he lowered himself slowly down into the room below.

As soon as he reached the floor, he made for the nearest word-processor and began to type. Behind his back, one of the toy soldiers emerged from the open doorway into the library and stood observing him, its seeing-eye lens focussed upon his activities.

In the Control Centre, the Master hugged himself with glee and held his breath, watching two television screens simultaneously. One threw up the picture that the toy soldier was 'seeing' – the Doctor, in quarter-profile, busily typing a new addition to the story of Jamie and Zoe – while at the same time the other screen relayed the words as the Doctor wrote them: ' . . . *with a daring plan for their escape. The enemy had been finally defeated . . .* '

The Master chuckled in anticipation: 'Yes, yes – don't stop – go on!'

The Doctor, still unaware that he was being watched, stopped typing to read back what he had written: ' . . . *The enemy had been finally defeated – by –* ' He stopped and continued more slowly. '*Defeated . . . By – the –* '

Then he slammed both fists on to the machine, making

130

the keys seize up. 'No! I can't do it . . . If I write about myself – that will be the end of me!'

He turned, and found himself face to face with the toy soldier. Too desperate to feel alarmed, he addressed the Master directly through the camera lens on the soldier's helmet: 'A nice try, and I almost fell for it, didn't I? A moment longer, and I should have turned myself into fiction!'

Furiously, the Master thumped the desk in frustration, and shouted: 'Arrest that man! We shall play games no longer!'

But as the toy soldier lumbered forward, the Doctor was too quick for him. Grabbing the rope of hair he swung himself up and climbed hand over hand until he was standing on the flat rooftop once again.

Cursing under his breath, the Master decided to settle accounts with his adversary once and for all: he picked up his pen, and began to write.

But the Doctor was safe and sound for the moment – dusting himself down, and thanking his new-found allies.

Rapunzel smiled sweetly, as she coiled up her hair: 'Only too happy to be of assistance . . . '

The Doctor looked around for Zoe and Jamie – but they had disappeared. In their place, Gulliver sat, surrounded by the Edwardian children whom the Doctor had met in the forest, when they besieged him with their riddles and word-games.

Crossing to speak to them, the Doctor asked: 'Where are Jamie and Zoe? Have you seen them?'

Gulliver replied civilly: 'They had to make a departure – it was necessary.'

The boy in the Norfolk jacket and knickerbockers chimed in: 'They'll be back soon, don't worry.'

Then they crowded round the Doctor, all talking at once: 'What's been happening? What will you do? Is it a game? Can we all play? What are we going to do?'

The Doctor put his hands over his ears, protesting:

'Please! You must give me a chance to think . . . There must be some way out . . . There's got to be!'

At his desk in the Control Centre, the Master was writing swiftly, his pen skimming across the page. A satisfied smile crossed his face, as he paused to read through what he had just created.

'Jamie and Zoe realised at last that the Doctor was in fact the most monstrous and cunning villain. There was no punishment too severe for the crimes he had committed. It was for this reason, that they proceeded upon a plan to put an end to his nefarious activities . . . '

A sharp, insistent bleeping sound broke his train of thought, and he glanced up from his manuscript. A warning red light flashed, and the Master pressed a button, saying: 'Permission to enter . . . '

A moment later, Jamie and Zoe emerged from the darkness, walking towards him. They looked as if they were sleepwalking: their faces were completely blank, without expression of any kind.

A pace behind them, two White Robots followed as their escorts – although now that they had no minds or wills of their own, this was perhaps an unnecessary precaution.

'Ah, splendid, splendid.' The Master greeted them jovially. 'Come closer, my children.'

Jamie stood rigidly at attention, gazing straight ahead, and saying: 'You sent for us, Master.'

'Yes, indeed . . . Now then – you do know, don't you, what your friend the Doctor is really like? There is no possible doubt on that score, I trust?'

Zoe repeated like a bright schoolchild reciting her lessons: 'He is the most monstrous and cunning villain . . . '

Jamie echoed her dutifully: ' . . . Monstrous and cunning villain – no punishment is too severe for the crimes he has committed.'

Gleefully, the Master explained: 'Well done; you are word perfect . . . That is why I sent for you both. At this moment of crisis I need your assistance in a little scheme I have devised . . . I flatter myself that it is rather ingenious.'

'Tell us what we must do,' said Zoe.

'We won't let you down,' added Jamie. 'Give us our orders.'

'Very well, then . . . Allow me to read you a short excerpt from the story I am working on . . . '

He settled his glasses more firmly on his nose, and began to read aloud.

Still the storybook characters crowded around the Doctor, as he paced the flat roof, trying to cudgel his brains to produce a plan of campaign.

They all wanted to help him - not understanding his predicament in the very least, but feeling concerned and sympathetic at his obvious misery. Gulliver said: 'I understand, sir, that you are in an unhappy situation.'

Rapunzel shyly pressed the Doctor's hand: 'I wish there was something I could do . . . Isn't there *anything*?'

The Doctor forced a smile: 'I wish there were.'

Suddenly the Edwardian children exclaimed in surprise, calling out excitedly: 'Look! What is it?' 'I don't know . . . I never saw it before . . . ' 'Where has it come from?'

The Doctor followed the direction of their pointing fingers - and he too gave an exclamation of amazement. 'The TARDIS - by all that's wonderful!'

There it stood, comfortably settled in a corner between two ancient towers: the dear old dark blue police box - waiting and welcoming.

'I don't understand . . . Safe and sound - as if nothing had happened . . . ' Incredulously, the Doctor made his way towards it: still suspicious - still more than a little wary. It all seemed too good to be true . . . And then, as if to make everything perfect, the door opened - and Jamie and Zoe walked out.

They raced up to the Doctor and hugged him: no longer sleepwalking, they seemed to be their old selves again, talking and laughing at the same time.

'Doctor - it's so good to see you - are you ready to leave?' Jamie asked.

'The time has come,' Zoe added, smilingly.

'The time?' The Doctor repeated, not understanding.

'The time to leave,' she explained patiently. 'We mustn't stay here any longer.'

'Yes, but – how did you find the TARDIS?' the Doctor wanted to know.

Jamie shrugged the question off impatiently: 'We'll explain all that later – let's not hang about – come on!'

'Jamie's right – we can talk afterwards,' Zoe agreed. 'The most important thing is to get away . . . After, you, Doctor.'

They stood back politely to let him enter the TARDIS first. As he went in through the door, he was saying: 'It's amazing – just as I was beginning to think we'd never get free – I was afraid it was all over . . . '

'Oh, no,' said Zoe sweetly, shutting the door quickly as soon as the Doctor was inside. 'It's not all over, Doctor . . . Not yet.'

And then she looked at Jamie – and giggled.

They heard a cry of horror and betrayal from inside the false TARDIS – and then the Doctor's voice was drowned in an electronic hum that built up to an ear-splitting climax. The front wall of the TARDIS fell down with a clatter, disintegrating as it collapsed into cardboard, canvas and gimcrack – like the scenery in a pantomime.

Behind it, the Doctor was a prisoner, trapped within a glass box like a specimen in a museum: with steel clamps round his wrists and ankles, and a steel collar encircling his throat . . .

The storybook children ran up for a closer look at this strange phenomenon: from inside his prison the Doctor saw their faces pressing close to the glass, to get a better look – their noses and cheeks flattened and distorted into hideous shapes, like the masks of gargoyles . . . He closed his eyes, to shut out the awful spectacle.

The electronic hum continued to build, and become an unbearable roaring – and the glass box, with the Doctor inside it, slowly faded from sight – leaving nothing but an empty space.

134

Well-satisfied with his work, the Master put down his pen and made a brief announcement into the microphone before him: 'The children have obeyed perfectly. Their mission is completed.'

He pressed another button, then turned sideways in his swivel-chair, knowing what he was about to see.

A space in the wall of computers and other busy electronic mechanism started to glow with an eerie blue light. The light throbbed in regular pulses, and shapes began to emerge within the space: slowly they joined together and created an outline – a silhouette – which acquired features and took on recognisable identity . . . The blue light convulsed and gathered itself into a sheet of glass – and there, a helpless prisoner within the glass wall, was the Doctor . . . At the heart of the computer.

'Splendid . . . ' beamed the Master. 'Now, perhaps, we can get down to business.'

10

The Doctor Has the Last Word

The Doctor moistened his lips: unable to move hand or foot, he was almost at the point of despair – and yet he had to persevere . . . He had to try and understand . . .

'Why are you doing this to me?' he asked, hoarsely. 'What is the purpose of it all?'

The Master sighed, and sounded genuinely regretful as he replied: 'You refused to take over my position here, at the controls – so we are forced to incorporate you into the computer itself. From now on, your brain-power will provide the creative force that is required to carry out our masterplan.'

'And what exactly is that master plan? May I be allowed to know?'

'Since there is no way that you can prevent it happening – I see no harm in confiding in you.' The Master smiled, a shade wistfully. 'It is a luxury for me, to have someone I can talk to . . . Yes, I will tell you, Doctor – our aim is to bring the whole of the planet Earth, and its people, under our command.'

'To destroy them?'

'No, no, not at all . . . We have no wish to destroy them – merely to adjust their minds to suit our purposes . . . You have seen for yourself how we dealt with Jamie and Zoe – they are not destroyed, but have been translated into another dimension, where they can be put to good use.'

'As your fictional puppets . . . ' The Doctor shuddered. 'And this is your intention – to subjugate the entire race of Earthmen in the same way?'

'Quite so. In due course, they will all become fictionalised – happy creatures, without pain or problems – '

'Sausages!' the Doctor interrupted bitterly. 'Mankind will be just like a string of sausages – all the same!'

'Mankind is only too keen to achieve that state of perfection,' the Master pointed out. 'Look how eagerly they all try to follow the same fads and fashions – "keeping up with the Joneses", they call it.'

The Master gazed mistily into the future, enthusiastically outlining the scheme.

'Earthmen and Earthwomen are so fond of fiction: they love to be told stories – in books, and plays, and magazines, in the cinema or on television . . . Thanks to the wonderful supply of never-ending fantasy that we shall be able to provide, fiction will become everyday reality . . . Gradually, they will lose all contact with the world around them – then they will begin to vanish from the earth, and reappear here.'

'Leaving the Earth undamaged and uninhabited, for you and your "higher powers" to take over, I suppose?'

'Precisely . . . I knew you would appreciate the plan – so vast in its implications, and yet so simple in its inception.'

'So simple – that it all depends upon my co-operation?'

'It no longer requires co-operation on your part. You have no choice, my dear Doctor: you are now part of the Master Brain.'

The Doctor could see that two new terminals had been linked to the giant, floating brain within the control computer – and he realised that these led directly to his own prison cell.

'So . . . Your computer feeds off my thoughts?'

'That is correct.'

'Then whatever I think – the Master Brain will create? In other words, in the final analysis, *I* am in sole charge?'

'No, no!' The Master looked quite shocked. 'You mustn't say such things – you are under our control!'

'Are you so sure?' The Doctor saw a gleam of hope. 'Might it not be the other way around? You were unable to control my mind before – remember? I doubt whether you can do so now.'

The Master rapped angrily on the desk before him and commanded:

'You will submit to a higher power!'

'*Never*!' The Doctor concentrated his thoughts, and prepared for a life-or-death struggle. His body might be in fetters, but his mind was still free and independent. 'You have given me equal power – now it's a battle of wits between us!'

The giant brain began to change colour again – throbbing from pink to a lurid orange, as it poured more and more mind power into the circuit.

'Stop this!' The Master cried desperately. 'Stop it at once!'

But the Doctor wasn't listening to him: he knew what he had to do.

'Jamie, Zoe, can you hear me?' he called, from the depths of his glass box. 'You must think for yourselves! Don't be afraid – you *can* open the book and find freedom . . . You *can* get out. Go on: try hard!'

The Master slumped back into his swivel-chair, moaning: 'This is against everything we have worked for . . .'

As his eyes closed, his face changed and became cruelly inhuman: in the clipped, metallic voice, he rapped out orders: 'Warning, warning . . . Emergency action – immediately!'

At the same time, the Doctor continued to send out thought-messages to his young friends: 'Don't be concerned with fiction – reality is all that matters now – you've got to hang on to real life . . . You've got to get out!'

The metallic commands boomed through every loudspeaker in the Citadel: 'Calling White Robots . . . All guards to report to Control Centre instantly . . . The Master Brain must be protected!'

From his cramped position within the wall of the computer, the Doctor could just see one of the television monitors beside the Master's desk – and with a sudden leap of excitement he recognised the scene that was being shown on the tiny screen . . . Jamie and Zoe using all their strength to push apart the heavy covers of the book that had imprisoned them.

'Keep going!' he called to them, encouragingly. 'You can do it – push harder – you've got to break out! That's the way – that's splendid!'

The printed pages opened up slowly, and Zoe and Jamie fought their way out of fiction – back to real life.

Simultaneously, a strange little scene was taking place up on the roof, where the storybook characters clustered around the two youngsters, who were slowly changing from cardboard creations back into flesh and blood.

'What is it?' asked the Edwardian schoolboy. 'What's happening to you? Is it a game?'

Gulliver looked at them with a kind of half-remembered recognition, and said sadly: 'We are no longer in the same service.'

Rapunzel tried to touch Jamie – and found that she could not.

'How horrid. You are going away from us,' she said.

The giant brain was now changing colour again – from orange to an evil, sulphurous yellow – and the Master rocked from side to side in an agony of frustration, seeing his plans beginning to disintegrate.

'Soldiers – to the roof – immediately!' he barked. 'Destroy the aliens!'

'*No*!' The Doctor shouted. 'Jamie – Zoe – run for it!'

They tried to escape – but the toy soldiers were coming at them from all sides.

'Back, Zoe!' said Jamie tensely.

Zoe appealed to the characters who surrounded them: 'You were our friends – can't you help us?'

'Alas, we obey our creator,' said Gulliver. 'That is all that can be expected of any character . . . Unless the Master bids us otherwise.'

The toy soldiers advanced steadily, keeping step as they closed in on their young prisoners. There was no escape.

The Master curled his lips in a sneer of triumph. 'Now, Doctor – you *will* obey.'

'Never,' said the Doctor. 'I am here to create fiction, you say? So be it – I will create . . . '

And he began to improvise, dictating rapidly: 'In this moment of crisis, when all seemed lost, the Karkus suddenly appeared – coming to their rescue.'

It was getting quite crowded on the rooftop, by now, but when the Karkus materialised out of nowhere in a blinding flash of light, they all stepped back instinctively to make room for him.

With a swirl of his cloak, he made a deep obeisance, saying: 'I . . . am . . . at . . . your . . . command.'

The Doctor continued the narrative as swiftly as possible: 'He raised his anti-molecular ray distintegrator and destroyed the soldiers . . . '

Obediently, the Karkus aimed his plastic pop-gun. A series of explosions followed, and the toy soldiers staggered back, toppling over, one on top of another – tumbling down like . . . a line of toy soldiers.

The Master watched this new development with horror, and snatched up his pen, beginning to write: 'But then the Karkus realised his mistake – he knew that he had been tricked. He had to face his real enemies . . . And turned his gun upon Jamie and Zoe.'

The Karkus followed instructions, and turned to face the young travellers: they found themselves looking into the muzzle of his space weapon.

'Look out, Zoe!' yelled Jamie. 'Duck!'

The Master scribbled on: 'With Jamie and Zoe fixed in his sights, the Karkus pressed the trigger – '

At once he was countered by the Doctor, who completed the sentence for him: ' . . . But the power of the weapon had failed completely: the gun was useless, and he threw it away.' (He added with a grin: 'You'll have to do better than that, my friend!')

'Tchah!' The Master redoubled his speed: his pen raced across the paper. 'Suddenly a swashbuckling figure appeared – poet and swordsman, the famous Cyrano de Bergerac . . . Remorselessly Cyrano advanced upon those who had dared to poke fun at his nose . . . '

'Just a minute – my turn!' gasped the Doctor. 'Cyrano found himself face to face with a fearless musketeer, that prince of duellists, D'Artagnan!'

On the roof, Jamie and Zoe turned their heads from left to right and back again, as if they were spectators at some surrealist tennis-match. From one end of the battlements, Cyrano brandished his sword threateningly, while from the other side D'Artagnan leapt to their defence, ready to do or die with his flashing rapier.

As fast as one champion appeared, another materialised to out-match him – when Cyrano seemed to be on the ropes, the Master switched characters – duelling-swords weren't lethal enough: he'd have to introduce cutlasses . . . ' 'Cancel Cyrano – substitute Blackbeard the Pirate!'

D'Artagnan found himself unarmed, as the hefty thwack of a heavy cutlass knocked his sword from his grasp, and the bloodthirsty buccaneer loomed above him, laughing coarsely as he raised his weapon to deliver the death blow.

'Cancel D'Artagnan!' snapped the Doctor. 'And substitute Sir Lancelot – in full armour!'

As the cutlass swung down D'Artagnan was replaced by an imposing figure clad from top to toe in steel and chain-mail. The sword hit it with a resounding clang, and Blackbeard staggered back, dropping his weapon and nursing his bruised fingers.

Amid all this confusion, nobody noticed that Jamie and Zoe had slipped away. They found an open dormer window in a sloping roof, and scrambled inside: they knew they had to find the Doctor, and rescue him before it was too late.

But perhaps it was already too late – for the metallic voice of the computer, speaking through the mouth of the Master, was issuing a new command: 'The Doctor must be stopped . . . He is expendable . . . Destroy him.'

The Master opened his eyes, and exclaimed in dismay, in his own mild, elderly tones: 'Oh, no – don't do that – he's the only person I can entrust with my job – I can't go on forever . . . Give me one more chance, please!'

Then his eyes closed, and the giant brain changed from yellow to a poisonous green, as the metallic voice thundered: 'You have failed: The Master Brain must be protected against any overloading . . . Robot force will deal with the enemy . . . Set Robot weapons to destructor beams.'

From his glass case, the Doctor saw the White Robots moving in for the kill: and the ribbed lenses which they usually held had now been replaced by wicked-looking pointed objects . . . As he watched, these objects opened up like the petals of a steel flower – and at the heart of each 'flower', where the stamen might have been, he saw the deadly pinpoint of a laser gun, trained upon him.

'Remove him from captivity.' The commands rolled on remorselessly: and the glass panel that boxed him in slid away – while the metal fastenings that bound his neck, wrists and ankles sprang open. He was free at last – free to step forward and meet his doom.

'Oh, my goodness – I must think . . . ' he told himself. 'How can I write myself out of this? Let me see: "As the White Robots advanced upon the Doc – " ' No, I can't say that!'

141

He caught himself up in the nick of time – once again, he had almost converted himself into fiction: that was not the way out.

Unseen, Zoe and Jamie had tiptoed into the Control Centre, and stood watching and listening – appalled by the situation. 'What can we do?' Jamie whispered. 'We can't fight those brutes on our own.'

'No, but didn't you hear what the Master said?' hissed Zoe. 'That computer bank controls everything here – and it's dangerously near to overloading . . . So let's overload it!'

The Doctor was now backed up against the giant brain, and the Robots held their laser weapons poised, ready to fire.

'It is a pity to destroy a mind as intelligent as yours, Doctor,' said the Master, 'but you leave us no alternative . . . Very well: take aim – disintegrate!'

The White Robots lifted their guns – and as they squeezed the triggers, Zoe dashed to the control unit and began to press all the buttons, one after another.

At this point, everything seemed to happen at once. The Master screamed: 'Stop her! She will wreck our plans – '

The Robots swung round, undecided, uncertain which order to obey. The Doctor seized his opportunity and made a flying leap for the control desk, helping Zoe as she punched up every function of the computer, sending the entire operation into a frenzy of whirring and clicking and flashing: tapes unwound, revolved, unspooled – upon the television screens a score of images danced crazily – the Karkus scaling a cliff . . .

But these snatches of fiction had all slipped out of gear: the unicorn galloped the wrong way – the Medusa retreated instead of advancing – the Karkus was climbing backwards . . . The overloaded computer had been thrown into complete chaos, and was running in reverse.

The giant brain turned black, and a gibbering voice tried to take control, repeating again and again: '*Destroy – destroy – destroy!*'

Totally disorientated, the Robots fired their laser guns at

random: several of them were aiming in the direction of the computer, and in a series of blinding flashes, whole banks of apparatus went up in flames.

In the middle of this carnage, the Doctor put his arm around the Master's shoulders, who lay motionless, slumped across his desk. Then the Doctor remembered the two electrodes plugged into the old man's skullcap, and quickly removed them.

The old man stirred and opened his eyes: 'Where am I? What's happening?' he asked faintly.

'Jamie – give me a hand – help me get him to his feet,' the Doctor panted.

'What do we want him for?' Jamie asked. 'He's the one who caused all the trouble!'

'Don't argue – there isn't time – just do as I say.'

Zoe went to their assistance, and between them they managed to drag the old man away from his desk, out of the centre of the holocaust.

One explosion after another rocked the library and on one of the television screens, where the picture was still running backwards, a tiny image appeared: the TARDIS, as it had been at the moment when it exploded and fell apart. Now, in reverse sequence the various fragments flew together, dropped into place, resumed their accustomed shape . . .

The Doctor, half-carrying the old man, was on his way out of the library with his companions close behind him – and they all stopped short as they turned a corner and found their own beloved TARDIS waiting for them. The light on top was winking and blinking: which meant there was no time to be lost. They opened the door, and went in – into the real TARDIS this time.

Gently, the Doctor lowered the old man into a chair; he looked about him in mild amazement, like someone waking from a dream, and said: 'Dear me – I'm not altogether sure where I am . . . Is this the office of *The Ensign* magazine?'

He had become a frail, harmless old gentleman once more, now he was no longer part of the computer circuit. The Doctor tried to explain: 'You were kidnapped, just as we were – they have been using your mind . . . But now – with any luck – we'll try to get you home.'

'Do you really think we'll get away?' Zoe asked, as another explosion, louder than all the rest, rocked the TARDIS upon its base. 'What's happening out there?'

'That depends how efficient the Robots are. I rather hope that at this moment they're all fully occupied in destroying one another – *and* that hideous giant brain as well!'

'But what about Gulliver and the Karkus and all our friends?'

'Zoe, do try to think clearly. Our friends are all fictional characters – they'll go on existing in their own dimension. You can't blow up a fictional character, can you? Their stories will last for ever . . . But for the time being, I think it's time to call a halt to this particular story . . . Jamie, make ready for take-off.'

The old gentleman in half-moon glasses still looked a little dazed. 'I don't quite follow – have I got to finish off another story?'

'No, sir, not this time . . . ' said the Doctor. 'If you'd allow me, I'll simply add the last word . . . '

And as he switched on the powerful drive-motor that would take the TARDIS off on yet another journey, he spelled it out for them:

Finis – or, if you prefer it –
THE END